PRAISE FOR DEEP FREEZE

"Susan Morris is at it again, ignoring the dangers of snooping around the tony underworld of Dubai. In Anne O'Connell's gripping new novel *Deep Freeze*, Susan probes the injuring of her friend Dr. Barry Thornton and stumbles on an evil cabal preying on domestic workers. Steeped in both cultural immersion and medical research, *Deep Freeze* is a gripping page-turner that builds to a crescendo of tension."

> \- Peter Moreira, author of The Haight Mystery Series

"What happens on a ski hill in one of the hottest places on Earth launches intrepid Susan Morris on a new—and potentially deadly—investigation. The Dubai ex-pat ultimately finds her way inside a hospital research lab where she uncovers illegal activity, cryogenics, and pure greed. All while her fifteen-year marriage is crumbling around her. Chillingly good."

> \- donalee Moulton, author of *Hung Out to Die*

"If you can't put *Deep Freeze* down once you start reading it, join the club. Anne Louise O'Connell's twisting and fast-paced plot and heart-thumping suspense will keep the reader up long after everyone else has gone to sleep. It's a masterpiece in criminal suspense, a whodunit that will keep you guessing to the very end. If I had to describe it in one word, it would have to be 'riveting.'"

> \- Vernon Oickle, award-winning journalist and best-selling author of 39 books, including the Crow series

"*Deep Freeze* is an engaging read on several levels. It's a well-written mystery that gently and then rapidly unfolds, offering insight into the ethical and moral dilemmas of domestic workers and the elite class of Dubai. The protagonist, an American ex-pat nurse, finds herself at the center of a major, all-too-plausible medical coverup. It leaves her and the reader breathless in the intrigue. This novel is a wonderful follow-up to the author's equally immersive mystery *Deep Deceit*, which is also set in the Arab world."
- Bruce W. Bishop, author of *Grow up, Rory Rafferty*

PRAISE FOR DEEP DECEIT

"*Deep Deceit* is compulsive reading from start to finish with a gripping storyline filled with tension and masterfully brought to an edge-of-the-seat crescendo. O'Connell cleverly combines the thrill of the chase with intense psychological elements, as her characters unravel under the pressure of events beyond their control. Who is telling the truth? What secrets does domineering husband, Ryan, hide, and how far will those in power go to avenge the wrongs he has done? Can anything save his wife and daughter? And where does love fit into this riveting tale? I couldn't put it down until all had been revealed."

- Jae De Wylde, author of *The Thinking Tank* and *Sleeping People Lie*

"Anne O'Connell has written an intimate thriller from an unusual and fascinating point of view: the families of Westerners living and working in the Gulf States. She takes the *Not Without My Daughter* plot and adds a new and satisfying twist."

- Tim Brookes, president of the Endangered Alphabets Project

DEEP FREEZE

DEEP MYSTERIES
BOOK TWO

ANNE LOUISE O'CONNELL

OC Publishing

*In loving memory of our Mother Theresa,
fondly known by all as MT*

CHAPTER
ONE

He snapped his flight bag shut, and she felt a jolt like paddles to her heart. Susan had watched her husband do this a thousand times, probably more. He had been a pilot as long as she'd known him. It just didn't seem to get any easier.

"Remind me again, where are you going?" She reached up and buttoned his top button and clipped on his tie, trying to prolong his inevitable departure. "I did look at your schedule, but I can't pronounce half the names of the places you fly."

"Christchurch," Mitch said. "How hard is that?" He smiled at her and leaned down for a kiss. "It's in New Zealand. Check it out on the world map in my office."

"Yeah, I guess I should."

Mitch shrugged. "Remember, it's a three-day trip. We go from there to Perth, then to Sydney, and back to Dubai."

"Okay. I'll miss you." Susan chewed her lip.

"Me too." He pulled up the handle on his roll-aboard suitcase and set his flight bag on top. "You have anything fun planned for while I'm away?"

"I'm meeting some EWG ladies at Ski Dubai later this morning. Pat and I are actually going to ski, and the others will be having brunch and mimosas at Café St. Moritz where we'll join them for après-ski. It should be fun."

"What's EWG again?"

"It's the expat women's group where I met Pat, remember? 'The ladies who lunch' and other stuff, like fundraising for local charities."

"Oh yeah, right."

She walked him to the door and picked a miniscule piece of lint off his jacket. Mitch turned and Susan stood on tiptoes to receive his kiss goodbye. His six-foot-two, slender frame was a stark contrast to her own petite, yet stocky build. It only added to her image of him as "protector." At only five-foot-four, she had to stretch to run her hand over his recently buzzed, blond crew cut.

"Have a good flight and call me when you get to the hotel."

"I always do." He turned and winked at her as he walked down the driveway and handed his bags to the driver's outstretched hand. "Have fun skiing," he called and waved as he climbed into the back seat.

Susan waved back as the driver pulled away.

A large emperor penguin scooted across her path, almost tripping her. Susan smiled and marveled again at the winter wonderland that had been created in the middle of a shopping mall in one of the hottest places on Earth. She remembered reading a news article about the first chick to hatch in the penguin habitat. She wondered if this one was the mom or the dad of the little wonder. Ski Dubai was one of the many over-the-top attractions the Emiratis had built so the city could rival any other destination in the world. This was her favorite of the "nowhere else on the planet would you see this" phenomena that preoccupied the thoughts and actions of the leaders of Dubai and the whole of the UAE, she figured. There was the tallest tower in the world; the biggest shopping mall, housing the largest aquarium ever built, where you could scuba dive with a plethora of exotic and dangerous marine life; and, of course, the biggest, most ornate mosque in Abu Dhabi.

Susan pondered these man-made wonders as she rode up the chairlift with her friend Pat, who was in silent contemplation as well—but from fear. It was only her second time on skis.

"You doing okay?" Susan asked and touched Pat's hand gripping the bar that ran across the front of them.

"Yeah, I'm fine." Pat smiled, still staring straight ahead. "Or, I will be once my feet are back on the ground. I really don't like heights."

"You'll have to let go of the bar before we can dismount, you know." Susan laughed and saw Pat loosen her grip. "Okay, here we go. Remember what we practiced last time. Put both poles in your left hand; I'll raise the bar, and as your skis touch the ramp, stand up and push off on the chair behind you with your right hand."

Pat nodded and squinted in concentration.

"Ski straight forward until we clear the ramp, and then we'll curve slightly to the right to the top of the run. Okay?"

Pat nodded again and took a deep breath as Susan lifted the bar over their heads. The chair reached the ramp and the two women stood up simultaneously, the chair gently nudging them from behind. They coasted down the small incline and swerved to the right, and Susan reached for her friend's elbow and pulled her to a stop to keep her from heading down the run before she was ready.

"See, that wasn't so bad, was it?" Susan put the straps of her poles around each of her wrists.

"Sure, but if you hadn't grabbed my arm, I'd be halfway down the hill by now, and probably flat on my ass."

Susan laughed and stomped her skis to get the excess snow off. She bent down and readjusted one of her boot buckles. "Isn't that Barry mashing moguls on the black diamond run?" She pointed to the one expert run—it was short but difficult, narrow and dotted with tall mounds of snow.

"Yes, it is." Pat sighed. "I forgot it was his regular day on the hill. He's here Wednesday mornings like clockwork. I probably wouldn't have come if I'd remembered. I wanted to surprise him with my prowess on the powder. But never mind. I'm sure he'll see us soon enough."

They both watched as his tall, lean form easily maneuvered the moguls, with each pole planted exactly where he needed it to be to launch hi' over the next bump. *He approaches it with a surgeon's precision*, Susan thought.

"I don't know how I'm ever going to keep up with him on the slopes in Austria." Pat let out a huff. "I wish we could have stuck to scuba diving again this year. I was just getting the hang of maintaining my buoyancy." She glanced down at her rather ample bosom and chuckled. "But, it's still several months until the Christmas holidays, and we did buy all new skiwear. A bit bright for my taste, but the ski patrol will be able to see us a mile away."

"They are pretty flashy. I like the purple and orange neon on Barry's," Susan said. "But you won't need rescuing. You'll be just fine. We'll have plenty of opportunity to practice before you go. Mitch is on a three-day trip right now, and I've got lots of time on my hands with little to do." Susan wasn't working, hadn't been since she and Mitch had moved to Dubai two years ago.

"Oh, I know it's going to be great. And I really appreciate the help. You're an excellent teacher."

"So people tell me. I just really enjoy it and am happy to help. I'm having fun too." Susan bit her tongue before adding that it was a cakewalk compared to the skiing she was used to in the Rockies, especially in Colorado, her favorite place to ski. She and Mitch had gone there every year before they moved to the Middle East.

"I'd hug you but I'm just trying to keep my balance in these things," Pat said as she strapped her poles around her wrists. "I need just a minute until my heart rate slows down."

"No worries." Susan wished Pat would just relax and get going. "Just take a few deep breaths." She inhaled and exhaled to demonstrate. "No need to rush. Ready whenever you are." Susan crouched in a racer's stance. "Better make it a good one, though. All the ladies are in the window at the café, watching."

"Oh, shit," said Pat under her breath. "Well, I guess we're the sideshow today. Might as well give them something to laugh about. We can make them buy us a round of fuzzy snowballs when we're done."

Susan laughed as she pushed off, thinking about the reward of her favorite libation after a day of skiing—hot chocolate with Grand Marnier. But it really wasn't the same when the temperature outside was over forty degrees Celsius. *More than a hundred Fahrenheit!* she thought. Even after all this time outside the US, she was constantly doing the conversion in her head. She wondered how high the electric bills were to keep the indoor ski hill so cold, especially during the summer months. She knew as soon as they exited the hill itself into the mall, the chill in the air would dissipate a bit, even though the mall was air-conditioned. She'd probably stick to a mimosa.

Susan managed the slope gracefully as she planted one pole after the other, demonstrating a gentle slalom for Pat. She had been skiing practically since she could walk and came regularly to Ski Dubai. It wasn't the Rockies, but it would do. She made a turn and stopped at the lip of the next section of the run and watched as Pat slowly made her way, alternating between a semi-proper turn and a snow-plow, which was what Susan had taught her to do any time Pat felt she was out of control. Being able to control even that movement was great progress.

Pat dug her skis into a deeper V as she approached Susan.

"You're doing great," Susan called to her and gave her a thumbs-up.

Just as the words were out of her mouth, Pat's tips crossed and she tumbled headfirst into the snow, coming to a rest at Susan's feet.

"Well shit!" She looked up at Susan. "I thought I had it."

"You did." Susan sideslipped downhill to give her friend some space to maneuver and to provide a brace in case she started sliding. "And now you get to practice getting up on an incline."

"Great." Pat scowled then laughed and moved her skis parallel to the hill as Susan had taught her, then planted her downhill pole firmly into the snow, put both hands on the top of it, and pushed down to bring herself to an upright position.

"Well done!" Susan clapped her gloved hands. "Now sidestep down until you're beside me."

Pat repositioned herself next to Susan with a wide grin of accomplishment on her face.

A loud pop reverberated through the cold air. Susan turned toward the sound and saw one of the chairs on the lift detach from the main cable. As it crashed down, she saw a flash of purple and orange.

CHAPTER

TWO

"Ladies and gentlemen, there has been a malfunction of the chairlift and the hill will be closing. Please make your way carefully to exit number 2B at the far side opposite the lift, next to the penguin habitat." The loud speaker crackled. "Do not stop or interfere with safety personnel. If you are injured, please plant your poles in the snow and cross them to form an *X*, and one of our rescue team members will be with you as soon as possible."

Susan's arm was around Pat's shoulder. She didn't know whether her friend had seen that Barry was on the chair that crashed.

"Oh my God, Susan, what just happened?" Their backs were to the lift, and Pat strained against her skis to try to turn around so she could see.

Susan reached out as Pat stumbled. "Hang on." Susan held tight to her friend's elbow. "You're going to twist a knee if you don't turn properly."

"Please exit as quickly and safely as possible," said the disembodied voice through the speakers.

"Okay, we need to get down the hill," Susan coaxed while trying to shield Pat's view.

Pat pulled her elbow from Susan's grip and crossed one ski over the back of the other and stomped down to release her binding the way Susan had taught her. With one foot free, she managed to turn and face the nightmare scene unfolding just below where they were standing.

"Oh my God, were there people on that chair?" Then she screamed, "No!" She tried to bolt, but her one remaining ski dug in and she lurched forward.

Susan reached out to grab Pat's arm but missed. Pat went down, her ski still attached to her boot. The ski lay at an awkward angle to her leg. Susan quickly released her bindings and knelt down next to Pat who looked at her with wild eyes and struggled to get up.

"Pat, stay still." Susan held her shoulders down. "I think you might have twisted something when you fell."

"But, Barry . . ." Pat began and then went limp.

Susan quickly pulled off her hat and neck warmer and put them under Pat's head. She reached for her ski poles and jammed them into the ground, tilting them toward each other to form an X. She released the ski still attached to Pat's boot, unzipped the bottom leg of Pat's ski suit, unclipped the boot buckles as gently as she could, and slipped off the boot. Pat groaned. There was already significant swelling. There was no bone protruding, but still, it wasn't good.

"Can I give you a hand?"

Susan was so focused on Pat she hadn't heard the on-hill paramedic ski across to them.

"Oh, yes, thanks." She stood up. "I think she has at least a bad sprain, but it could be a break."

The paramedic was already forming a splint around

Pat's left leg. He reached for the rescue toboggan and pulled out a backboard. "Can you help me get her onto the stretcher? My partner is busy with other injured skiers. I'll talk you through it."

"Of course," Susan said. "I'm a nurse so I know how to transfer to a backboard."

The two managed to get Pat onto the toboggan, and the paramedic stood and braced the extended handles between his elbows and sides. He had just started a careful sideslip down the hill when Pat regained consciousness.

"What happened?" she asked, trying to sit up. "Susan? What's going on? Where's Barry?" she called.

Susan was keeping pace beside the toboggan as best she could, carrying both her and Pat's skis. "Everything's going to be okay," she said with more confidence than she felt. "I'll check on Barry and let you know what I find out."

"No, I need to go to him." Pat clawed at the straps across her chest.

"Pat, you're hurt and need to go to the hospital," Susan said.

As they approached the exit, the paramedic stopped and clicked off his skis. "There are ambulances waiting. We're taking everyone who has been injured to the American Hospital in Al Barsha," he told Susan. "I'm sorry you can't ride with your friend, but you can meet her there."

Susan nodded, already headed toward the lockers to change.

THREE

Susan ran into the emergency room and up to the reception desk. She quickly scanned the waiting room and the hallway opposite the Plexiglas that separated the waiting room from the ambulance bay and didn't see any stretchers. She was hopeful Pat and Barry had both been admitted and were being seen.

"Please, I'm looking for my friends who were just brought in from the accident at Ski Dubai. Can you tell me where they are?" Sweat trickled down her back under her turtleneck.

"One moment and I'll check for you." The receptionist turned to her computer. "What are their names?"

"Barry and Pat Thornton. He's a doctor here and Pat's his wife."

The receptionist looked up. "Are you family?"

"Um, no, but they don't have any family here. I'm a close friend."

"I'm not supposed to release any information to non-family members."

"Okay, I understand." Susan paused. "But I was with Pat when the accident happened, when her husband fell. She'll be so worried. Is there a way to get a message to her that I'm here?"

"Well, considering the circumstances . . ." The receptionist looked back at the screen. "It looks like Mrs. Thornton is up in X-ray. Take the elevator to the third floor and there's a reception desk to the right as you exit. You can ask there if you can see her."

Susan dashed to the elevator. "Thank you so much," she called over her shoulder.

On the way up she thought about Pat and Barry's story, shared with her over many lunches and glasses of wine. They were such a power couple in Dubai. He a star surgeon at a world-renowned hospital, the very one he'd been brought to, and she a skilled fundraiser and event planner. They were both Canadian and had met when Pat was working for an event company organizing a symposium on international research collaborations. Barry was attending along with classmates who were doing general surgery residencies at the University of Western Ontario. The two fell in love and got married soon after.

For the first few years Pat had continued to work in Toronto while her husband worked with Médecins Sans Frontières in Iraq and Syria and commuted back and forth. A former professor of Barry's was working in Dubai and encouraged him to apply for an opening at the American Hospital there. Pat had told Susan that Barry needed a break and was missing her, so he convinced her that there would be lots of opportunity for her in Dubai. They decided to take the leap, and Barry applied for and was offered the position. Pat gave up her job and followed him to the other side of the world.

Susan knew what that was like. She had done the same. She had already been taking a break from nursing when Mitch proposed leaving the US, where they had both lived their whole lives, and moving to the Middle East. It would be an adventure, he said. It certainly was an adventure— and an ongoing culture shock for Susan, even after two years of expat living.

She burst out of the elevator, blew past the reception desk, and followed the signs directly to the medical imaging waiting area.

"Susan?" a weak voice called out.

She turned and backtracked to the open door of a smaller waiting area where Pat, on a stretcher, was the lone occupant.

"Oh Pat! I'm glad I found you."

"Oh my God, Susan." Pat reached for her. "I'm so relieved you're here." She tried to sit up and Susan gently pushed her back down. Pat resisted. "Have you seen Barry? What's going on? I need to know!" Again, she tried to get up, but Susan's hand was on her shoulder.

"I know you do and I'll do my best to find out," Susan reassured her. "For now, you have to let them take care of you."

A technician entered the room and reached out to read Pat's admission bracelet.

"Okay, Mrs. Thornton, I'm going to take you to X-ray now, and then we'll get you settled in a room. Your friend can wait in the bigger waiting room down the hall, and we'll let her know where you'll be."

"My husband, Dr. Thornton, do you know where he is and what's happening?"

"I checked on that for you, and I believe he's in surgery. One of the nurses has gone up to get more details for you and will hopefully know more when you're done here."

"Susan, can you please find out? I need to know he's okay." Pat clung to Susan's hand.

"I will," Susan promised. "You just get yourself taken care of, and I'll meet you back here when you're done. Or, if they have a room for you, I'll find you."

Susan waited until Pat was wheeled into an X-ray room and the door closed behind her. She had to find out what Barry's condition was before Pat lost her cool. She knew that as a surgeon at this very hospital, he would be given the best care. She wouldn't doubt it if the hospital's head of surgery was in the operating room right now, taking care of one of their top surgeons himself.

Even though it had been a while since she had worked as a nurse, she was very comfortable in the hospital surroundings. She tried not to dwell on the circumstances that led to her leaving her last position. It was a long time ago, and she needed to focus on getting an update on Barry's condition. She scanned the sign between the elevator banks and found Surgery. It was on the next level up. She headed for the stairwell, too impatient to wait for the elevator, and took the stairs two at a time. She paused at the landing on the fourth floor and took a deep breath, steeling herself for bad news. She shook her head to clear the image of the twisted metal of the chair and Barry's brightly colored ski suit dropping through the air. In order to get the information she needed, she would have to maintain her composure.

She walked onto the surgical floor and marched with purpose to the nurses' station.

A nurse looked up from the tablet she was holding. "Can I help you?"

"Yes, I hope so. Dr. Barry Thornton was in a terrible accident and has been brought here, and I'm told he's in surgery now. His wife is in X-ray and has asked me to find out how her husband is doing."

"Of course." The nurse put the tablet down and stood. "One of the nurses from X-ray was just here, and I told her Dr. Thornton was still in surgery. You just missed each other. They messaged me from downstairs and told me to expect you. If you'll just have a seat over there," she pointed to a row of chairs along the wall, "I'll see if I can find out how much longer he'll be in surgery."

"Do you know the extent of his injuries?" Susan asked, relieved to know Barry was still alive.

"I'm sorry, I don't," she replied. "Please take a seat and I'll find out what I can."

Susan had been pacing the hallway for what seemed like hours. She was just about at the end of her patience, when she saw the nurse who promised to bring her an update coming toward her.

"How is he? I've had several texts from Mrs. Thornton asking about her husband." She refrained from asking what had taken so long. She knew from personal experience how busy the nurse must be.

"I really can't tell you anything other than he's out of surgery and in recovery. Why don't you see if Mrs. Thornton is finished in X-ray and bring her up?"

"Okay, I'll do that, thank you."

Susan fought down her frustration, knowing Pat would be sick with worry. She pushed open the stairwell door and tore down the stairs.

She approached the X-ray reception desk.

"I'm looking for Mrs. Thornton."

"She's in the small waiting room," the receptionist said, pointing down the hall. "They haven't assigned her a room yet. We're waiting for an ortho to take a look at the X-rays."

"Great, thanks." Susan headed down the hall to find her friend.

Pat was fuming in a corner of the waiting room when Susan entered. "What the hell, Susan? What took you so long?" She tried to stand up from her wheelchair, winced, and fell back. "Jesus Christ." She slammed her fist on the arm. "Bloody ankle!"

"I'm so sorry, Pat. It's been hard getting any real news, other than he's out of surgery—"

"Well, I have to go to him, now!" Pat tried to stand again and cried out.

"Pat, you have to stay seated or you're going to make your injury worse," Susan said, hoping to calm her friend. "Did they say if your ankle is broken? Or whether it's a sprain or torn ligament?"

"I don't give a shit," Pat yelled. "I just want to see Barry." She started crying.

"Of course," soothed Susan. "I'll take you up now." She flipped off the brakes of the wheelchair and spun Pat around and out the door.

"I'm taking Mrs. Thornton to see her husband," Susan said as they passed the reception desk. She punched the elevator up arrow and the doors opened.

"That could be a problem if the ortho comes to follow up and she's not here," the receptionist shouted after them.

"I don't care, I need to see my husband," Pat called out as the elevator doors shut.

Susan wheeled Pat toward the nursing station on the surgical floor. She paused when she saw a tall, lanky doctor in blue scrubs coming out of a recovery room.

"That's Dr. Pettigrew, Barry's boss," Pat said. "He's also from Ontario, but we didn't know him there."

In a few long strides, the doctor had reached them.

"Pat, I was told you were here," he said, holding out his hand. "It's good to see you. I'm so sorry it's under these unfortunate circumstances."

"Frank, how is Barry? Can I see him? Did you have to do surgery?" Pat started crying again. "I need to see him, Frank. Please. Where is he?"

"I know you are eager to see your husband, but let's just sit for a minute and I'll explain everything." He held his hand out to Susan. "Dr. Frank Pettigrew."

Susan shook his hand. "I'm Susan, a good friend of Barry and Pat's." Her stomach fluttered and grumbled ever so slightly. She hadn't eaten since breakfast. "As you can tell, Pat is anxious for an update."

"I understand that. She can see Barry in just a minute." He sat in a visitor chair and motioned them over.

Susan wheeled Pat over and handed her a tissue.

Dr. Pettigrew took a deep breath. "Pat, your husband is in critical condition. He had internal bleeding, but we were able to get it under control." He paused and took her hands in his. "Both of his legs are broken, but they are clean breaks and they will heal fine. He also has a broken collarbone and a few broken ribs. We have stabilized him, but the main concern is the head injury. From what we can gather, his helmet flew off at impact, which caused a brain bleed. We relieved the pressure of the bleed and were able to stop it, but we're not sure of the extent of the injury. We won't know for a few days. He's in a medically induced coma to keep him calm while the swelling comes down. We are doing everything we can, and I am personally overseeing his care. He is a valued member of our team, and we want to see him recover fully."

"Can I see him?"

"Of course." Dr. Pettigrew stood and motioned for Pat and Susan to follow. As he led them down the hallway, he explained, "We usually only let family go in, and one at a time. But considering the circumstances, your friend can take you in." He smiled at Susan and pointed down a short hallway that jutted to the right. "His room is the first door on the right, the only one. My office is just back where we came from, so I'll be close." He put his hand on Pat's shoulder. "I'll check in later."

"Thank you, doctor," Pat said, and Susan turned the wheelchair and pushed it toward Barry's room.

Upon entering they were bombarded by the beeping of machines monitoring his vitals and the whoosh and hiss of the ventilator helping him breathe. Pat choked back a sob as Susan pushed her right up to the bed.

"Barry?" Pat whispered and reached over to take his hand. She lowered her head onto his arm and wept.

Susan put her hand on her friend's shoulder and squeezed. "I'll be right outside," she said and quietly left the room.

She softly closed the door behind her and made her way back toward the main corridor. She could hear angry voices, and when she turned the corner she saw Dr. Pettigrew leaning over the nurses' station desk, shaking his finger at the duty nurse. Susan bristled remembering the domineering doctors who had tried to demean her in her nursing days. It was unacceptable. She clenched her fists, took a deep breath, and marched toward the station. Her motion caught their attention, and the doctor straightened and cleared his throat.

"I want to be kept apprised of Dr. Thornton's condition and be paged immediately if anything happens. I'll be back in a few hours," he said to the nurse.

"Yes, Dr. Pettigrew," the nurse answered politely, then she busied herself with paperwork on her desk.

"Dr. Pettigrew," Susan called. He turned to her. "I just wondered, there was someone else on the chair with Barry. I was told they brought all the injured parties here. Do you know how they're doing?"

"Yes, it was an anesthesiologist who works here at the hospital. He's in pretty bad shape. If you'll excuse me, I have a surgery scheduled shortly."

He turned on his heel and retreated down the hallway. Susan sighed and headed back to Barry's room. She was partway there when she heard a high-pitched cry.

"Susan! Nurse! Anyone! Please come!" called Pat.

Susan broke into a run and burst into Barry's room.

"What's happened?" Susan asked just as the duty nurse blew in.

"I swear he was awake," Pat stuttered, her breath coming in huffs. "He . . . he was . . ." Her tears were flowing.

"Okay, sweetie," soothed Susan. "Take a deep breath."

"He looked right at me and tried to say something." Pat wiped her nose with her arm. "And he squeezed my hand really tight."

Barry moaned and rolled his head back and forth on the pillow.

"See!" Pat cried. "He's just squeezed my hand again. That's a good sign, right?"

The nurse was checking the monitors on the opposite

side of the bed from where Pat sat in her wheelchair, trying to stay clear of the wires and tubing snaking their way into her husband's arm and attached to the ventilator tube and the sensor pads stuck all over his chest.

"His heart rate is a bit elevated but nothing to worry about. Still, I'll page Dr. Pettigrew just to be sure," the nurse said and quickly left the room.

Barry's eyes opened and he turned to his wife. He lifted his free hand, made a fist, and raised it up to his head.

Then his eyes closed and his hand fell back to his side.

"Barry, honey, open your eyes," Pat whispered. "What are you trying to say? What do you need? I love you. You're going to be fine." She kept whispering in his ear, in between sniffs.

Susan pulled up the visitor's chair next to Pat's wheelchair. "I think it's too soon for him to be coming out of the induced coma," she said, and put her arm around Pat's shoulder. "The swelling on his brain needs time to come down. But it is a good sign that he opened his eyes."

As Susan soothed Pat, Dr. Pettigrew walked in, the nurse at his heels.

"He opened his eyes, did he?" Dr. Pettigrew pushed a few buttons on one of the monitors and flicked the tube running out of an IV bag and into Barry's arm. "Anything else?"

"Um . . . he was making a motion with his hand," Pat said as the doctor moved to her side of the bed and wedged himself in beside her wheelchair. "He made a fist and brought it up to his head." She demonstrated the hand motion her husband had done.

"If you can move back just a bit, I'd like to check a few things."

"And he squeezed my hand, twice," Pat added as Susan pulled her wheelchair back.

Dr. Pettigrew grabbed a small flashlight from his lab coat pocket, clicked it on, and lifted Barry's eyelids one at a time, shining the light into his eyes. He took hold of Barry's hand. "Dr. Thornton? Barry? If you can hear me, squeeze my hand."

They all waited in silence, amidst the beeping and whirring of the machines.

"Well, his pupils are responsive but sluggish, but that's to be expected." Dr. Pettigrew sighed and rubbed his eyes. "All we can do is wait and hope things keep improving." He turned to the nurse. "Please give him another dose of pentobarbital. I was just about to scrub in for my surgery and have to get back, but keep me posted."

"Yes, doctor," the nurse replied.

"You should get some rest, Pat." Dr. Pettigrew put his hand on her shoulder. "It won't do your husband any good if you collapse from exhaustion. If you need anything to help you sleep, I can write you a prescription."

"Thank you, Frank, but that won't be necessary." Pat wheeled herself up to the bed again. "And, I'm not leaving." She took her husband's hand and laid her head on his shoulder.

Susan followed the doctor out into the hallway.

"I'll make sure she's okay," she said. "I'll go get her some food."

"Good idea. Hopefully she'll eat it," Dr. Pettigrew said. "And she should take care of that ankle. I saw the X-rays. It's not broken, so she doesn't need to be admitted, but she probably needs it wrapped and something to bring the swelling down."

"Okay, I'll mention that to her," Susan said. "I'm a nurse so I can take care of wrapping it."

The doctor murmured something and started punching and scrolling on the tablet he was holding. He grunted, turned away, and headed down the hallway, his mind obviously elsewhere already.

Jerk, Susan thought and punched the elevator's down button to go to the cafeteria.

CHAPTER
FOUR

Susan pulled into her driveway at eight o'clock the next morning, exhausted. The dashboard display told her it was already thirty-eight degrees Celsius. There was no respite from the oppressive heat of the Arabian desert surrounding them on three sides. The fourth side was the Persian Gulf, a body of water that brought no relief. There were no refreshing breezes coming off the water, and taking a dip didn't bring the cooldown effect that a splash in the Atlantic or Pacific Ocean did. Most of the year it was like swimming in soup. Her regular beach boot camp was suspended during the hotter months, so she had to rely on her rowing machine and other indoor workouts to stay in shape and the odd run at sunset when it was slightly cooler. She would have to find a gym that offered Pilates. She gave herself a shake. She needed to stop obsessing about working out. There were more important things to focus on.

It was hard to believe it had been less than twenty-four hours since the horrible accident that put her friend's husband in a coma. Unable to convince Pat to go home to rest, the nurses had moved a cot into Barry's room so she could at least stretch out, although she insisted she wouldn't sleep. Knowing she wouldn't leave his side, Susan had brought her a sandwich, which had gone untouched. She had also picked up some anti-inflammatories and a wrap for her ankle. Pat had allowed Susan to administer both but only after Susan stood her ground and insisted. Fortunately, while Pat was waiting in the ER, they had put an ice pack on her ankle, which had taken the worst of the swelling down. Susan didn't want to leave Pat alone, so she had slept on and off in the visitor's chair. She finally left to go home to shower and change, with a promise to return. Pat had received several messages from some of the EWG ladies who had witnessed the accident but she wasn't up to seeing any of them.

Susan switched off the engine and got out of the car. She left her ski gear in the back, too tired to carry it into the house. She approached the front door of their lovely, one-level, ranch-style bungalow, provided by her husband's company, in a compound that housed only EmAir employees. It was a great perk, and Susan loved the area and her neighbors, who were from all over the world. On one side were fun-loving Brad and Joan from Zimbabwe, and across the street were fellow Americans Wanda and Harold. She had also befriended an Irish gal and a couple of ladies from Kenya whose husbands were all pilots, so they understood the stress and pressure of the ongoing testing and evaluations their husbands endured while learning new routes and training on new aircraft.

As she unlocked the door and entered the foyer, her phone started to vibrate. She looked at the caller ID and punched the answer key.

"Hey, honey, I'm so glad you called." Susan dropped her

keys in the bowl on the credenza by the door and plunked herself down onto the bench next to it.

"I was hoping you'd be up," replied Mitch. "I've got a pickup in a couple of hours but wanted to hear your voice before I headed out. What's up? You sound frazzled. Did Pat's ski lesson not go well yesterday?"

"Oh, Mitch, that's the understatement of the century." Susan's voice caught in her throat, the stress of the previous day catching up to her. She started to weep.

"Sweetheart, what happened? Are you crying?"

Susan took a few deep breaths. She had been holding on all day and night for Pat, and now that she was in the comfort of her own home, the reality of what had happened hit her like an out-of-control freight train.

"Okay, now you're worrying me. Susan? What's going on?"

"Shit, Mitch, I don't even know where to begin. Hold on a minute." She switched to speakerphone, set her phone down, and pulled a tissue out of her purse. Amidst sniffling and blowing her nose, she explained as best she could everything that had transpired.

Mitch whistled. "God, Suze, I don't even know what to say."

"I know, isn't it awful?" She blew her nose again. "Watching that chairlift crash to the ground and realizing Barry was on it, I thought I was going to puke. And poor Pat. She's totally wrung out. Understandably so, right? She's still at the hospital. I just came home to get some rest and a shower. Or maybe a bath. And somehow fit in a workout before I go back to the hospital."

"That is awful, honey," Mitch agreed. "Seems these things tend to follow you."

Susan thought she heard him chuckle. "Excuse me?

What's that supposed to mean? And what's so funny?" Her tears were replaced by puzzlement.

"Well, Suze, are you forgetting last year, when you got embroiled in that situation with your friend Celeste?"

"That 'situation' was her daughter going missing," Susan snapped. "And I didn't get 'embroiled' in it, I was helping a friend. Like I am now. They wouldn't have found Tamara if I hadn't stepped in. The police certainly weren't any help." The last line came out through gritted teeth.

"I'm sorry, I can hear that I hit a nerve," Mitch said, trying to soothe. "I don't mean to sound heartless, and I hope Pat's husband will be okay."

"His name is Barry. Dr. Thornton, actually. He's a surgeon," she said. "You'd know more about him if you had come with me when we were both invited to dinner, rather than claiming to be too tired." Susan stopped herself before she went too far into her regular rant about making new couple friends. She sounded like a broken record, even to her own ears. She sighed. "It's really too early to tell whether he'll be okay or not. He's still unconscious and on a ventilator, but they've started weaning him off, and the doctor said he would come later today to hopefully take it out. Barry did open his eyes at one point yesterday and squeezed Pat's hand, which is a good sign."

"That does sound like a good sign, and it sounds like you went into full nurse mode," Mitch said. "I think you should reconsider getting back into nursing." He paused. When Susan stayed silent, he continued. "I know you said you were never going back, but it's been a while now since, um, you know. We've been in Dubai for almost two years, and there are so many opportunities for nurses . . . "

"Mitch, I don't want to talk about it. You know it upsets me, so why do you even bring it up?"

"It wasn't your fault." He hesitated. "And it's how we met. You were so good with Stan, and—"

"I said I didn't want to talk about it!"

"Okay, I get it, but jeez, you're such a great nurse. I'm just saying." He stopped. "I'm sorry to leave our conversation like this, but I've got to jump in the shower and study the flight plan again before pickup. We can talk when I get home tomorrow."

"I'm not sure if I'll be here or not," Susan answered. "I want to be at the hospital when they take the ventilator out, and I'm not sure when that will be. Text me when you land in Sydney."

"Okay, I will. And, I'm sorry I—"

Susan disconnected the call before Mitch could finish. She couldn't believe he was being so callous. It was so unlike him to be insensitive to Pat's situation and to bring such a painful memory back for Susan. Her experience working as a psychiatric nurse was a mix of good and bad memories. She and Mitch had met in the psychiatric facility where his brother, Stanley, was a long-term resident. It was hard now for Mitch to be so far away from his brother, but his parents were there and visited Stan regularly, although they were getting older and finding it more difficult. Susan knew at some point Mitch would probably have to take over the power of attorney and Stan's health directive from his parents.

Her mind jumped to another patient and that mind-numbing phone call she had received from a co-worker. Susan had been changing out of her scrubs after a long shift when she got the call about a patient who had really gotten to her. He had been working through some childhood trauma and suffered from dissociative amnesia. The news that he had died by suicide floored her. His doctor had told her just that day that their patient was making progress, and she had spent the afternoon chatting with him. What had she said that could possibly have sent him over the edge? And where had he gotten the box cutter he'd used to slit his wrists? So many questions and no answers. The family had filed a lawsuit for wrongful death but had eventually dropped the case. Her boss had stood by her and reassured her it wasn't her fault, but she felt the horrible weight of guilt and knew she could never go back to nursing for fear of negatively impacting another human being.

Susan shook off a sense of foreboding, went into the bathroom, and turned on the tap to fill the tub. She would add some essential oils to help calm her nerves so she would be refreshed for her return to the hospital. She had to be strong for her friend. She dropped her clothes on the floor, lit the candles on the counter, switched off the light, and climbed in. She took a deep breath, paused, then immersed herself under the water and exhaled, sending bubbles to the top.

FIVE

Susan's phone buzzed as she pulled into a parking spot at the hospital. She put the car in park and looked down to see a text from Pat.

— *The doctor is on his way. They're about to take the ventilator out. Where are you?*

She texted back.

— *Just parking. Be right there!*

She reached into the back seat and grabbed her jean jacket; even wearing a turtleneck at the hospital yesterday, she had almost frozen. She knew they kept the temperature at minus-frigid degrees because it kept the bacteria down, but visitors didn't get heated blankets like patients did.

When the elevator doors opened on the surgical floor, Susan caught sight of Dr. Pettigrew turning the corner to Barry's room followed by a nurse. *Great, I'm not too late*, she thought as she picked up her pace. When she entered the room, Pat was stepping back from the bed. No longer in a wheelchair, she was relying on a boot the orthopedic surgeon had recommended and a cane that was lying across the visitor cot, which had been pushed off to the side.

The ventilator was still huffing away on the opposite side of the bed, breathing for Barry. Dr. Pettigrew acknowledged Susan's entrance with a nod and turned to check Barry's pupils, then placed his stethoscope on Barry's chest. Barry was still unconscious, but when the doctor moved to the end of the bed and ran a blunt metal object across the soles of Barry's feet, they each showed a positive response with a downward flex.

Dr. Pettigrew looked at Pat. "Are you ready?" he asked. "It's not pleasant and Barry may cough and choke a bit, but that's normal. It won't hurt but it's damn uncomfortable."

"Are you sure he's ready to come off of it? Will he come to right away?" Pat asked.

"Yes, I'm sure he's ready," the doctor answered. "His vitals are good and we have him on minimal support already. It's not likely he'll come around right away—he's still sedated."

Susan put her arm around Pat and gave her a reassuring squeeze.

Dr. Pettigrew turned to the nurse. "Ready, Carolyn?" The nurse nodded and moved in front of Pat and Susan as the doctor turned off the machine, removed the tape holding the tube to Barry's face, took a firm grip of the tube, and pulled in sync with Barry's inhalation then exhalation. Barry coughed and gagged and the nurse immediately suctioned inside his mouth.

They all waited. Susan held her breath and prayed. The monitors continued to show a steady heart rate, and Barry's chest continued to rise and fall.

"Okay, that's it for now," Dr. Pettigrew said as the nurse gathered the used tubing, which she wrapped in a blue pad and tossed in a bin in the corner. "I'll check back later." He turned to Pat. "You should get some rest. It's up to Barry now. His body needs time to heal."

"I can't leave him," Pat whispered.

"Very well, but he wouldn't want you to get sick, which is what will happen if you don't take care of yourself. I know it's hard but . . ." He shrugged his shoulders, then turned to the nurse. "Let me know if anything changes."

"Yes, doctor," she said and followed him out of the room, closing the door behind her.

Pat pulled up the visitor's chair and resumed her position at her husband's side, holding his hand. Susan put her hand on her friend's shoulder. She had to find a way to convince Pat to take a break but knew it was futile to even try just yet.

"Oh my God, Susan, look!"

Barry had opened his eyes and was raising his hand to his face, this time with thumb and pinkie extended.

"Barry! You're awake." The tears were flowing freely down Pat's cheeks. "What are you trying to say?"

Barry groaned and his head rolled slowly from side to side on his pillow. He croaked out two words through cracked lips. "Iiiii ffffunnn."

"Honey, I don't know what you want. Are you in pain?" She turned to Susan. "Go get the nurse. Hurry!"

Susan turned to go then stopped, hand on the doorknob, as Barry's voice came through clearer and stronger.

"Mmmaaa fffone!!" he managed to get out. His eyes were wild.

"Relax, my love," Pat soothed and stroked his arm. "I'll get your phone but you shouldn't worry about that now. You need your rest."

"Nnnnoo . . . nnnnow." He struggled to get the words

out. "Please!" The last word shot out like a cannon, then his eyes closed and he went limp.

"I'll get the nurse," Susan said quietly. "He's so agitated he probably needs more sedation. We also need to notify Dr. Pettigrew. I'll be right back."

She quickly found the nurse who paged Dr. Pettigrew then returned to Barry's room, right behind Susan. The nurse was checking the monitors when the doctor rushed in.

"What happened?" he asked and pushed in front of the nurse. "Sorry, Pat, can you please move back?" She had barely gotten out of the visitor's chair when Frank pushed it out of the way. Susan caught Pat's arm as she stumbled, awkward with the boot on her foot.

Barry's eyes flew open again and he grabbed Frank's arm. "N-n-not . . ."

"Not what, Barry? Don't worry, I've got you. It's going to be fine." He turned to the nurse. "Two milligrams of lorazepam" was all he needed to say. The nurse was already preparing a syringe and administered it into the IV port.

Barry relaxed again and whispered something as he fell into a sedated sleep.

"Did he say, 'not accident'?" Susan asked.

"I couldn't really tell. He was mumbling. And probably hallucinating." Frank busied himself checking lines and pressing buttons on the monitors. "He's had too much stimulation for one day. You really need to let him rest. Only family visiting from now on." He glared at Susan.

"Susan is family." Pat linked her arm through Susan's. "I want her here. I need support. I don't have anyone else here, and I can't do this by myself."

Dr. Pettigrew mumbled something that sounded like agreement before adding, "He'll be sleeping now for a few hours, so you might as well go home and get some rest. Or at least a shower." He crossed his arms, raised his eyebrows at Susan, and nodded toward the door.

Susan narrowed her eyes at him but knew he was right. She could see he wasn't going to leave before they did anyway. "He's got a point, Pat." She took her friend gently by the shoulders and looked her in the eyes. "Let's let Barry rest, and we'll go and get his gear at the ski hill. His phone is probably in his ski bag. If you have it next time he wakes up, that will calm his nerves."

Pat nodded and her shoulders slumped. "Okay, but I need to come right back."

"Fine. After we get Barry's things, I'll take you home so you can have a shower and change your clothes. Then, I promise, I'll bring you back."

Dr. Pettigrew was handing Pat her cane when the door opened and a man barged in. He was wearing a grey three-piece suit and otherwise looked like a WWE wrestler, barrel-chested with a thick neck.

"Ah, Dr. Pettigrew," he said, holding out a hand that looked like a ball glove.

Frank shook the extended hand. "Hello, Mr. Becker. I assume you're here to check on Dr. Thornton. Good of you to come." He turned to the women. "This is Pat, Barry's wife, and Susan, a family friend. Ladies, this is our hospital CEO, Alex Becker."

"Good to meet you," the CEO said and shook their hands. Susan detected a German accent.

"Nice to meet you too," she said.

"We did meet once before," Pat said. "At a welcome cocktail reception when Barry first started work here."

"Ah, yes, nice to see you again." He turned to Frank. "How is our star surgeon doing?" he asked. "I was at the ER bay when they brought him in. Made sure they knew how important a patient he is. Escorted him right to the OR myself. I was glad to see you were handling the surgery. Any complications?"

Frank seemed to bristle at the question. "Surgery went well and we've been able to remove the ventilator. He's resting now and we expect a full recovery."

"Ah, very good," Becker said. "We can't have him off for too long now, can we?" He laughed and clapped Frank on the back.

Susan cringed and turned to Pat, raising her eyebrows.

"We should go and give him some peace and quiet," Frank said ushering the crowd out of the room. "He needs his rest."

"Yes, of course," Becker said. "We want a speedy recovery, don't we, Mrs. Thornton?"

Pat just nodded and took Susan's arm as they all exited Barry's room. The women made their way to the elevator, and the men stopped to have a conversation.

"He's an odd duck," Susan said as she punched the ground floor button.

"I'll say. He obviously didn't remember me, but I had very little interaction with him at that reception. He was busy talking to the 'right' people."

The women rode the elevator down in silence, each lost in her own thoughts.

Susan drove down the Palm Jumeirah, the breeze wafting freely through her Jeep. She loved driving with the doors and roof off but could only do so a few months of the year, as most of the time it was too damn hot. It was time to put them back on as the summer "breeze" wasn't particularly refreshing. Pat and Barry lived on the second last frond on the right, from where you could see the world-renowned Atlantis Hotel rising up from the sea like a kraken at the very end of the man-made, palm-tree-shaped island. The island was a feat of engineering that was in keeping with Dubai's mission to be the biggest and best at everything. The wow factor of the island blew Susan's mind every time she drove onto it. She marveled at the row upon row of apartment buildings on both sides of the raised roadway that was the trunk of the palm tree design. Each luxury high-rise had a stretch of white sandy beach that ran across the entire seaward side of the building, end-to-end decks overlooking the beach, and Olympic-sized pools and tiki bars. The trunk of the tree gave way to multiple fronds sprouting from either side that contained sprawling single-family homes, each with its own private beach and most with pools.

"It's so beautiful," Susan mused aloud. "I just can't fathom how they built it. You have to admire the sheikh for his vision and the city planners for making it happen."

Pat was silent in the passenger seat.

Susan put her hand on Pat's knee. "You okay?"

Pat shook her head.

"I know this is a lot to handle, but I'm here for you." Susan turned on her indicator and headed down Frond G. "Barry is going to be fine."

"But where is his phone? He's going to be so upset."

"It's probably in the house. He just forgot it or decided to leave it home while he was skiing. Don't worry, we'll find it." Susan felt a familiar prickle but shook it off. *Just a wayward hair tickling the back of my neck*, she thought. She ran her fingers along her hairline at the back and fluffed the dark curls that tumbled to her mid-back. She pulled into Pat's driveway and put the car in park. "You go ahead. I'll bring in his ski bag. His skis must have been damaged beyond repair—" She stopped and kicked herself when she saw the crushed look on Pat's face. "Can you manage alright with your boot and cane, or do you need help?"

Pat shook her head, swung both legs around, got out, and walked slowly to the front entrance.

Susan went around and yanked open the gate at the back of her Jeep. A scream came from inside the house, and she ran to the entrance. Pat was standing motionless in the foyer, her hand over her mouth, her cane on the floor. Susan walked quickly over to her friend and took in the shambles of the living room. Furniture was overturned and books were strewn all over the floor, the bookshelf emptied.

"Oh my God." Susan put her arms around Pat, who was shaking.

"Why?" Pat's strangled question came out in a whisper. She stepped away from Susan and yelled, "Anu!" She called out again, "Anu! Are you home?"

"Pat, sit down, you're going to reinjure your ankle." Susan guided her to the nearest upright chair. "You stay here; I'll look for her." Susan handed Pat her purse. "Call the police."

Susan hoped the Thorntons' live-in helper wasn't home —if she had been when the place was trashed, there was no telling what the perpetrators might have done to her. Susan knew how much Anu meant to them; she was like family.

Susan methodically checked every room in the villa, including the small cottage on the property that was Anu's. There was no sign of her. When she returned to the living room, Pat was still sitting where Susan had left her, holding her phone, staring into space.

"Pat? Are you okay?" Susan crouched in front of her with her hands on Pat's knees. "Did you call the police?"

Pat blinked and let out a heavy sigh. "Yes, they said they would come right away." Just as she was finishing her sentence there was a knock on the door. She looked at Susan. "Did you find Anu?"

"No, she's not here."

Susan stood and went to answer the door. The prickling sensation had returned, like an army of ants running across her neck.

CHAPTER
SIX

After taking hundreds of photos of the ransacked villa, dusting for fingerprints, interviewing both Pat and Susan, and asking a dozen times if Pat knew where her maid was, the police finally closed their notebooks and promised to get back to Pat if they got any leads.

For an hour after they left, Pat paced, with a shuffle of the boot and thump of her cane, from one end of the open-concept living and dining room to the other, chewing on her fingers and babbling to herself. Eventually, the lack of sleep caught up to her, and she finally gave in to Susan's insistence that she shower, eat something, and have a rest. Pat grumbled as Susan helped her cover her lower leg with a plastic bag to keep the boot dry in the shower. The grumbling continued as she closed the bedroom door behind her. Susan smiled to herself when she heard the shower turn on. She opened the bedroom door a crack and called in, "Let me know if you need any help."

"I'm fine, thanks," Pat called back.

Susan closed the bedroom door and hoped Pat would be

okay. It would be awkward showering with one foot off to the side.

Susan wasn't one to sit still. Usually when she was fidgety and distracted it meant she needed to exercise. She hadn't had time for it earlier, and she pictured her rowing machine sitting in the spare bedroom and itched to run home for a quick workout. But she certainly wasn't going to leave Pat alone as agitated as she was and with Anu missing. So while her friend showered, Susan righted furniture and gathered the books up off the floor.

The bookshelves anywhere Susan had ever lived were organized alphabetically by author, but she knew that not everyone was as particular as she. Mitch always gave her a hard time about her alphabetized spice drawer, but there were so many bottles, how else was she going to find what she was looking for? That's how she always defended her borderline obsessive tendencies to him and then pointed out his color-coordinated sock and underwear drawers.

After tidying up, Susan headed to the kitchen to see what she could put together. *Something simple and nutritious*, she thought. She opened the fridge and spied some spinach, an apple, and some blueberries. Now all she needed was some ginger and honey and she'd have a great green juice for the two of them. She put two eggs on to boil for sandwiches as well.

As she was getting the blender out, she heard the bedroom door open.

Pat shuffled into the living room in her robe, one foot bare and the other booted. "I really can't sleep," she said and dropped onto the couch Susan had set upright. "My mind is going a million miles a minute." She looked around. "Thanks for cleaning up." She closed her eyes and sighed. "You didn't have to do that. You should go home, be with your husband." She put her face in her hands, and her shoulders started to shake.

Susan sat next to her. "It's okay," she said, putting her arm around her friend. "I'm getting us a little bite to eat. Mitch isn't home until tomorrow, and I don't want you to be alone."

Pat sniffed and pulled a tissue out of the pocket of her housecoat. She blew her nose. "I wouldn't be alone if we could just find Anu." She scanned the room as if expecting to see the young maid lurking in a corner.

"Maybe she just went out grocery shopping," Susan suggested.

"If she had, she'd be back by now."

They sat quietly for a few minutes, both of them deep in thought.

Suddenly, Pat sat up like she was possessed and looked wildly around the room. She stood up and stumbled. Susan stood and took her arm.

"What's wrong?"

"Remember the police said to check around and see if anything was missing?"

"Yeah, I remember," Susan said.

"When you were cleaning up, did you happen to see a blue velvet box, about this big?" Pat held her hands roughly twelve inches apart.

"No, I don't think so." Susan paused to think again about all the items she had returned to shelves and to the dining room sideboard. "What was in it?"

"Oh God, oh God, oh God . . . no . . ." Pat sank back down on the couch. "I was holding an antique jeweled letter opener for safekeeping for the silent auction at the EWG gala." She got up again and hobbled over to the dining room. "It would have been here." Her hand flew to her mouth. "Oh, Susan, there was also a small Ming vase and a kintsugi bowl." She sat down and shook her head.

"Kintsugi?" Susan asked.

"Yes, it's a Japanese art form where they fix broken pottery and seal the cracks with gold or silver."

"I've heard of that." Susan sat down at the dining room table next to Pat. "It's about repairing something rather than tossing it away. Kind of reminds us to embrace our imperfections."

"How am I going to tell the committee?"

"Look, it's not your fault." Susan took her hand. "Someone broke into your home. They won't blame you."

"I can't deal with this. I need to get back to the hospital."

"Pat, don't you think you should rest? And I'm just making some sandwiches. You need to eat something. "

"No, I don't." Pat turned to face her. "I can drive myself. I'm not an invalid! I'm perfectly capa . . ." Her voice trailed off.

Susan looked down at Pat's hard-plastic-boot-encased foot and raised her eyebrows.

"Okay, fine, I can't drive." Pat huffed. "If you won't take me, I'll take a cab."

Susan started to speak, but the look Pat threw her made her close her mouth and think again. There was no sense fighting with her.

"Okay, fine." She gave in for the time being. "I'll take you back. But you're so wound up you're going to have a breakdown. This is a lot to process. Why don't you just stretch out for a bit? You can start a list for the police of what's missing. Let me fix you a drink to relax, and I'll finish getting lunch ready—a very late lunch, that is. I can't believe it's almost five o'clock!"

Pat nodded and shuffled to the kitchen to get a notepad and pen while Susan poured them each a double Scotch, neat. After handing one to Pat on the couch, she carried hers to the kitchen, made sandwiches, and blended her green concoction, which she put in the fridge for later. *It wouldn't mix well with Scotch*, she thought.

She handed Pat a sandwich and sat down beside her. Susan wondered if the intruders had still been in the house when she and Pat arrived. Perhaps their arrival had scared them off. She shuddered at the thought.

They sat quietly, munching on their sandwiches. Before long, Susan heard a soft snore coming from Pat. She rose and gently took the Scotch from her friend's hand, set it on the coffee table, and covered her with a blanket. Then she grabbed one for herself and curled up in the opposite corner of the couch and drifted off.

Pat was shaking Susan awake. "I can't believe we slept all night! Must have been the Scotch." She stumbled past Susan and headed toward her bedroom. "It's already nine o'clock. I have to get back to the hospital."

Susan sat up, rubbed her eyes, and pushed the blanket aside. "Okay, just let me get my bearings."

"There's an extra toothbrush in the powder room. Help yourself." Pat closed the bedroom door behind her.

Susan figured she best get her teeth brushed and be ready to go as soon as Pat reappeared. Susan would suggest they make a quick stop at her place to put the doors back on the Jeep. She knew the missing doors made Pat nervous, especially on the highway, and she didn't need the extra stress.

Even with the stop, Susan and Pat arrived at the hospital before noon. They went straight to the fourth floor, bypassed the nurses' station, and headed down the corridor. Ahead of them, at the end of the hallway just before the turn to Barry's room, they saw two women, heads close together in serious conversation. One was wearing hospital scrubs, the other was in street clothes and a colorful headscarf.

"Anu? Is that you? Is everything okay?" Pat called down the hallway.

The woman in the headscarf turned toward them then quickly followed the other who had disappeared around the corner.

Pat started hop-walking as quickly as she could, still hampered by the boot. "Anu?" she called. "Stop, please."

Susan hurried ahead of Pat, rounded the corner, and pushed open a door across from Barry's room that had just clicked shut. She looked down an empty hallway that ended with double doors with a sign that said, *Restricted. Hospital personnel only.*

"Where did they go?" Pat was out of breath as she caught up to Susan. "Damn boot! I should just take the damn thing off!"

"You can't do that if you want your ankle to heal." Susan leaned against the door, propping it open. "They've just disappeared through those doors." She pointed down the hall. "I guess we can't check in there. Or, maybe we can?" Susan started down the corridor.

"Wait, Susan. We probably shouldn't," Pat called after her. "But, I swear that was Anu. And the woman in the scrubs, did she look like one of Barry's nurses? Why would they run from us?"

They were both catching their breath when the woman

in scrubs came back through the double doors and approached them with a stern look on her face. Susan recognized her as Carolyn, the nurse that had assisted Dr. Pettigrew with Barry's ventilator, the same one he had chastised. She hadn't looked happy when Frank added Susan to the approved visitor list.

"Ladies, this is a restricted area." She motioned for Susan and Pat to move back through the exit and pulled the door closed behind them all. "I have to ask you not to wander the hallways." She started to wag her finger at them but instead clutched the stethoscope hanging around her neck. "This is a surgical floor, and the patients are all in recovery." She turned to Pat. "Your husband should be on another floor by now, but Dr. Pettigrew wants him close by." She put her hand on Susan's shoulder and gave a not-so-subtle push. "Now, please, either go into Dr. Thornton's room or leave the hospital."

"I'm sorry," Pat said. "I thought I saw you talking to my maid, Anu. I haven't seen her since my husband's accident."

"I'm afraid you're mistaken," Carolyn replied. "That was one of our cleaners. She's new and couldn't find where she was assigned for cleaning. I was just showing her the way." She reached for Susan again. "You shouldn't be roaming around the halls of this floor."

"She said we're sorry." Susan shook the nurse's hand off her shoulder. "Give her a break, why don't you?"

The nurse pursed her lips and shooed them farther from the exit door. "Dr. Thornton's sleeping now, so maybe you should come back later."

"No, I'm going to see my husband." Pat did an about-face and pushed open the door to Barry's room. Susan followed close on her heels and closed the door in the nurse's face.

The women smiled at one another. "Bitch," they said in unison and giggled.

"Hey, beautiful lady." Barry's voice was raspy but clear. He coughed.

Pat step-hopped to his side, took his hand, and brought it to her lips. Then she leaned down and kissed him gently on the mouth. "Oh, my sweet man, you don't know how good it is to hear your voice! I thought I'd lost you."

Tears welled then spilled down her face. Barry reached up to wipe her cheek and winced.

Susan hovered in the background, not wanting to interrupt the reunion. "With a broken collarbone it'll take a while for you to have full range of motion in that shoulder," she said.

"Hey, Susan." He coughed again.

"Hey." She walked up to the foot of the bed. "You gave us quite a scare."

"What . . ." He took a deep breath. "What the hell happened?" He pushed out the words then paused to take a few shallow breaths, struggling to continue. "I remember," he paused and took another breath, "being on the chairlift . . . The next thing, I wake up, and Frank . . ." He closed his eyes, seemingly gathering his strength. "Frank is hauling a tube out of my throat. Then . . . I think . . . I passed out."

"There was an accident," Susan began. "Um, the chair somehow disconnected from the cable of the lift and . . ." She stopped, not knowing how much he should hear. It was dangerous to upset him with his head injury.

"I th – think I re – remember that." Barry's speech started to slur.

"Don't strain yourself." Pat placed her hand on Barry's shoulder to calm him.

He squeezed his eyes shut and opened them again like he was trying to force himself to remember.

"You've had a traumatic experience, and it will take a while to heal and for your memory to become clearer," Susan said. "We should probably let Dr. Pettigrew, I mean Frank, know that you're awake."

"No . . . wait . . . my phone, did you get it?" he whispered.

"It wasn't in your ski bag," Pat said. "Don't worry about that for now. We'll find it. It's got to be in the house. Or, maybe in your office here?"

He shook his head and closed his eyes. "Ask . . . Anu . . ."

"Ask Anu what?" Pat looked at Susan. "Honey, ask her what?"

He opened his eyes again. "I just . . . need to . . . talk to her." He paused and took a ragged breath. "Need . . . the . . . file."

"What file? Barry, you're not making any sense. What does Anu have to do with anything? I don't know where she is." Pat's voice rose an octave and quivered. "There was a break-in at the house, and she's gone missing."

Susan shot Pat a look, hoping she would stop, knowing it was too much for him to deal with. Then she looked at Barry who had gone whiter than the sheet that covered him. He went limp.

CHAPTER
SEVEN

In the sweltering, late afternoon sun, the heat wafted up from the asphalt in ripples like a misty waterfall mirage. There were workers in blue coveralls crouched under trees or any overhang that threw enough shade to give cover. They clutched clear plastic bags filled with some type of juice, their fists gripping the gathered top as they sipped the liquid through a straw. The laborers who worked on the construction sites dotted around the city were mostly from India, Bangladesh, Pakistan, or Sri Lanka and tended to gather in country groupings. Many brought their lunches in layered tins. Each layer contained a different item—often rice, chicken, and broth.

Susan's heart went out to them. It must be unbearable to work outside in such oppressive heat. She wondered if their living quarters were air-conditioned; she doubted it. She had seen where many of them lived at the edge of the desert, in what looked like army barracks, and had heard stories of how many were crammed into the sparsely furnished rooms.

She watched as they headed back to work, some

swinging their empty canisters, others dropping their garbage in one of the many waste receptacles that were placed every ten feet no matter where you went in Dubai. Again, she questioned how they worked in the heat. All construction sites were supposed to shut down if the temperature went above fifty degrees Celsius, which it often did in the summer months, but even so, shutdowns were rare and there were reports of laborers fainting from the heat and falling from scaffolding. As Susan walked, she wondered why they wouldn't be wearing safety harnesses.

She had time to take this all in as she and Pat slowly crossed the parking lot. They weren't sure how long Pat would have to wear the boot, but thankfully, the sprain wasn't as bad as they first thought.

When Frank had come in to check on Barry, he was clearly upset with them and told them they had to leave and let Barry rest. He told Pat she was impeding her husband's progress, which Susan thought was unnecessarily cruel of him to say. Pat agreed to leave but was determined to return soon.

As they climbed into Susan's Jeep, Pat's phone dinged. She dug it out of her purse, and her hands started to shake when she looked at the screen. "It's Anu." She turned to Susan. "She's at home now and needs to talk to me but says not to tell anyone." Her voice cracked. "Will you come with me? She knows you, and I could use the support."

"Of course," said Susan. "I'm taking you home anyway." She reached over and squeezed her friend's hand. "Don't worry, I'm sure everything is going to be fine." But Susan wasn't so sure.

Both women were silent the entire drive to the Palm and onto Pat and Barry's street. When Susan parked in their driveway and took the keys out of the ignition, Pat sat still and didn't make a move to take off her seat belt. Susan reached over and unclicked it, then put her hand on Pat's knee.

"The sooner we go in, the sooner we'll find out where she's been." Susan smiled. "And what she knows," she added. "Come on, let's go in."

Susan walked to the passenger side and opened the door. Pat stared ahead. "I don't think I can." She started shaking. "Maybe they're having an affair."

"Oh Pat, that's absolutely not happening. Not Barry." Susan put her hand out. "Come on, let me help you down, and we'll get to the bottom of this together."

Pat reluctantly swung her legs over and grabbed Susan's outreached hands for support as she climbed down then grabbed her cane.

Pat fumbled with the keys, dropping them on the doorstep. Susan picked them up and opened the door.

"Anu, are you here?" Pat called out as she shuffled across the foyer and into the living room. "Anu!"

"I'm here, Madame, in the kitchen," a strained voice answered.

Susan led the way across the living room and looked toward the kitchen. A large island divided the spaces. At first, she didn't see the Thorntons' young live-in maid. Susan scanned the perimeter of the space and finally spied Anu sitting on a stool in the far corner, in a small gap between the double-wide fridge and the window. The blinds were turned down, completely blocking any outside view.

Pat pushed past Susan and stopped at the end of the counter, just a few feet from where her maid sat. She hooked her cane on the counter and put her hands on her hips. "Anu, what are you doing hiding in the corner?"

"Oh, Ma'am Pat, I'm so glad you're home." Anu hopped off the stool and ran to her. She threw her arms around her boss. "Is Dr. Barry okay?" she asked. "I'm so scared." She started crying.

Pat took Anu by the shoulders and held her at arm's length. "Scared of what?" Pat shook the girl. "Scared of what, Anu?"

"Pat, let her go and give her a chance to talk."

Pat's hands dropped to her sides and her shoulders drooped. She leaned against the counter.

Susan walked over and put her hands gently on Anu's shoulders. "Are you okay?" she asked. "We thought we saw you at the hospital today. Were you there?"

"Oh, Ma'am Susan, I don't . . ." She stopped, looked at Pat, and broke into sobs.

"Anu," Pat spat out. "Are you sleeping with my husband?"

"What?" Anu shook her head. "Oh no . . . no, of course I'm not. I would never . . ." She reached out for Pat's hand. "Please believe me. You are so good to me. I would never . . . " She took a shuddering breath, then exhaled. "I ask him to help find my friend," she began. "She went missing and I asked him. I thought maybe he could check at hospitals. Now he's hurt and they break into the house." She took another ragged breath.

"Who is 'they'? What do you know about the break-in?" Susan asked quietly, handing Anu a tissue.

"Nothing, I . . . I don't know . . ." She sniffed loudly then blew her nose. "I see strange men come up the beach, coming here. I don't think they are friends. They look mean and they don't knock, just open the door. I hear them say Dr. Barry is in the hospital. I run out the side door and hide in the bushes. I think maybe they take me if they find me, so I go to my friend next door and she hides me in her room."

"Oh, Anu, I'm so sorry." Pat reached for her and drew her in for a hug. "I didn't want to think those awful thoughts, but I was sure I saw you at the hospital earlier, and you ran when I called your name. I didn't know what was going on or what to think. I still don't." Pat released Anu from her embrace. "Did you happen to see Dr. Barry's phone anywhere? We thought it was in his ski bag, but it's not."

"No, Madame, I didn't. But I will look."

Susan noticed that Anu was avoiding the question about being at the hospital but decided not to push it.

"Why don't we all sit where it's comfortable, and I'll put on the kettle." Susan guided the two women into the living room. "Anu, take a deep breath and start at the beginning. What did you ask Dr. Thornton to help you with?"

Susan hurried up the walkway to her front door and let herself in. The living room light was on. Mitch had been home from his trip for an hour or so and had texted to say he'd wait up for her. She had meant to text him back but was too distracted with everything going on. She headed down the hallway quietly, not wanting to wake him if he was sleeping.

"Susan?" Mitch called from the bedroom.

"Yeah, it's me." She entered and made her way over to their shared walk-in closet where he was hanging up his uniform.

He reached for her and she walked into his arms and leaned her head against his chest and sighed.

"I'm glad you're home."

"Well, I'm glad I'm home too." He held her tight. "What's up? I texted you when I landed and didn't hear back. I sent a couple more texts but figured you were probably still at the hospital with Pat." He released her. "Or, you're still mad at me. Our call didn't end well yesterday. I was in a hurry and feel badly about how we left it."

"I'm sorry," Susan said. "It wasn't totally your fault. You were a bit heartless, but I'm just stressed and probably hypersensitive." She took the dress shirt he handed her to take it to the laundry room. "It's going to require a glass of wine or two to fill you in. Are you too tired, or can we talk?"

"I'm off tomorrow so I'm all yours," Mitch said. "Just let me finish unpacking my bag and I'll be right out to join you."

"Okay, I'll pour."

Susan melted into the corner of their big, overstuffed, L-shaped couch and crossed her legs, lotus-style. She gripped her large glass of cabernet sauvignon like it was a lifeline. The equally full glass she had poured for Mitch awaited him on the coffee table.

Mitch was wearing his favorite shorts and a baggy T-shirt with the Rolling Stones lips emblazoned on the front. He grabbed the other glass and situated himself in the corner opposite her and put his feet up on the coffee table, crossed at the ankles. Susan winced. He knew she didn't like when he did that, but she chose to let it go. There was too much else going on to nitpick on something small like heel prints on her coffee table. People's lives were at stake.

"Okay, I'm all ears," Mitch said, settling in.

"I really don't know where to start," Susan began.

"You're up to speed at least to the point of Barry's accident."

"Yes, I am." Mitch took a sip of his wine. "How's he doing?"

"He's off the ventilator and his vitals are strong, so he's going to be okay. It'll take some time, but he should make a full recovery." Susan shook her head. "It's amazing, really. For him to not have permanent brain damage after that fall. It had to be at least a hundred feet." She put her glass on the coaster on the coffee table and sat back. "He did come to briefly and said some pretty crazy things, though. And their home was broken into and ransacked, and their maid was missing until late this afternoon when she reappeared at their house."

"Whoa, that's a lot of shit going on." Mitch pulled his feet off the coffee table and sat up.

"That's not the half of it. Anu—that's their maid, a live-in who has been with them forever and is just like family. I may have mentioned her before. Anyway, Anu said she saw who broke into the house and thinks she knows why, or partly why, anyway. The police will want to question her at some point now that she's reappeared." Susan reached for her wine, sat back, and slowly swirled the red liquid around the bowl of her glass, the motion helping to calm her nerves. "We really don't know if there's a connection, but she told us she had asked for Barry's help in finding a friend of hers, Sara, who went missing about a month ago. Seems she was pregnant, and there are rumors going around that if a maid gets pregnant—or any single woman working here, really—they are deported for illegally having sex out of wedlock."

"I've heard that too," Mitch said. "I've operated flights where we're told there are maids being deported back to their home countries. The authorities escort them onto the plane, and they are met by local authorities upon landing."

"That's awful. Why didn't you tell me that?"

"It's just what's done," Mitch said and took another mouthful of wine. "We're living in a Muslim country, and if you don't follow the rules, there are ramifications. Just like you can be arrested for public intoxication or public displays of affection."

"But in this case, most of the time it's not their fault. Anu told us the employers are forcing the maids to have sex, and when they get pregnant, they get rid of them. Anu's friend said she was going home to Sri Lanka, but Anu said she never got on the plane."

"That's interesting. We do often have last-minute changes to the passenger manifest, and I have noticed a few times that there are maids who are being repatriated back to their countries who are removed from the list. I just figured they either got married or lost the baby or made a deal with their bosses." Mitch shrugged. "To be quite honest, I haven't put too much thought into it. I just keep my head down and do my job, which is stressful enough without worrying about some random maid's problems."

Susan suddenly felt nauseous. "Some random maid? That's pretty callous."

"Oh, come on, Susan, get a grip." Mitch put his glass on the coffee table and stood up. "You don't even know them. I know this sounds terrible, but it's none of our business." He tilted his head and sighed. "I see that look in your eyes, and I'm telling you, don't get involved."

"I'm already involved and I will not 'get a grip.'" Susan fumed. "I know Anu and it's her friend who has gone missing. I can't believe you can just turn a blind eye."

"I can because it means keeping my job." He started to

walk away then turned back. "I mean it, Susan. If you start digging around in places you have no business, you could jeopardize my job."

"But Mitch, these are my friends. Please understand."

"Well, I'm your husband and I won't have it."

"Is that right? Well, I make my own decisions," she said, surprising herself. She rarely contradicted him, but she needed to stand her ground. "I'm going to take a bath."

Susan stormed down the hall to their en suite bathroom, closed the door, and leaned against it. Why was Mitch being so cold? It wasn't like him at all. She turned on the hot water tap, added just a touch of cold, and dropped a bath bomb under the running water. She rummaged in Mitch's wash kit looking for the nice mini shampoos he always brought home from his layover hotels. Susan hadn't bought shampoo, body lotion, or soap since she'd been with Mitch. She found what she was looking for then froze. She pushed aside his toothpaste and pulled out a string of three small, flat, square packets. What was Mitch doing with condoms in his wash kit?

She flew out of the bathroom, into the living room where he was watching TV, and confronted him. "What the hell is this?" she shouted and threw the string of prophylactics at him.

"What? What do you mean?" He picked up the offending item and looked at it and then at her, seemingly confused. "Jeez, Sue, they just have these in the bathrooms at our layover hotels. It's nothing to get all upset about."

"That's bullshit," Susan spat. "I've never seen that."

"Of course you wouldn't. They know in advance when the wives are coming. I don't use them, but the other guys sometimes do."

"Then why the hell would you put them in your wash kit? We don't use them, I'm on the pill."

"I must have grabbed them when I grabbed the shampoo and lotion. Don't make such a big deal of it. I promise, I'm not cheating on you."

Susan let out a long huff of air. She was too tired to fight anymore. She didn't buy his story but was confused and angry and wanted to sink into a hot bath. *Oh shit, the bath!* She ran down the hall and got to the bathroom just in time before the tub overflowed. She needed to clear her head and get a good night's sleep. She would deal with it all in the morning. She gingerly lowered herself into the hot water then sank into the bubbles and let out a huge sigh as tears quietly coursed down her cheeks.

CHAPTER
EIGHT

When Susan awoke the next morning, Mitch wasn't in bed with her. She hadn't noticed if or when he had come to bed, but his side was ruffled so he must have. She swung her legs out from under the covers and padded barefoot out to the kitchen. There was a note on the table from Mitch saying he had gone to the gym. *Well, good*, Susan thought. She didn't really know what to say to him, and she wanted to get back to the hospital. Pat had texted to say she had taken a taxi and was already there and Barry was awake. Their drama would give her something to focus on as she tried not to let her imagination get away from her. She knew her husband was faced with so many temptations just due to the nature of his job; the flight attendants for EmAir, who were from all over the world, were the most beautiful people Susan had ever seen, male and female. She had heard the stories of what happened all the time between the pilots and flight attendants on layovers. She had always firmly believed that Mitch was too principled for that. Maybe she was over-reacting?

She shook her head and popped a bagel in the toaster and plugged in the kettle. She would make a quick coffee with the French press and take it in a to-go mug.

But first she needed to get twenty minutes of rowing in. She pulled on a T-shirt and a pair of shorts and headed into the spare bedroom. She turned the tension wheel to high and reset the foot pedals to her shorter leg length.

"Alexa, play 'In the Hall of the Mountain King.'"

The strains of Grieg's music flowed around her as she pulled and pushed, working up a sweat while trying to focus on her breathing and the music, eliminating any negative thoughts. Her mother had introduced her to classical music; she'd always had that or her favorite folk singers playing on the radio when Susan was growing up. As the music built to a crescendo, so did the intensity of Susan's workout. She recalled the day her parents died. The voice of the police officer who came to the house to inform sixteen-year-old Susan of her parents' deaths played in her head over and over. "There will be an investigation into the collapse of the bridge." He talked about "suspicious circumstances," but eventually it was deemed an accident. She shook off the sad memory, then smiled at the thought of her aunt, Margaret, who had taken in Susan and her two younger brothers. She should call Aunt Margaret and catch her up on the latest news . . . but not today.

The timer dinged at the twenty-minute mark, and she slowed to a stop. It was quick, but better than nothing. Now she felt ready to face her day—after a shower. She got undressed in the bathroom and averted her eyes from the mirror. She didn't need to see her body now. It only triggered a mental checklist of all the things she hated about it. No time for that today. She knew Pat needed her, and that was more important.

Susan pushed open the door to Barry's room and was happy to see the Thorntons holding hands, heads close in conversation.

Pat turned and smiled. "Hey, Susan, look who's awake." She turned back to her husband and kissed the back of his hand.

"Good to see you," Barry said. His voice cracked a bit.

Susan walked to the foot of the bed. "I'm so glad to see you awake and talking, though your voice is a bit raspy from the ventilator tube. You may be a bit dehydrated too." She walked to the bedside table and poured water from a pitcher into a glass. She bent the straw and held the glass in front of Barry's face.

Pat laughed. "Always the nurse. Frank was in earlier and said the same thing. More water."

"It's a hard habit to break," agreed Susan. She took a seat in the visitor's chair set back a bit from the bed. "Do you guys mind if I stay for a bit?"

"No, not at all," said Pat.

Barry nodded. "Pat just started telling me about the break-in," he said slowly, his voice raw. "A few things are missing, right?"

"Yes, a couple of auction items for the charity fundraiser I'm working on," Pat said. "I feel so awful."

"It's not your fault someone broke into your house," Susan reminded her.

"And you can't find my phone?" Barry asked. "It's not in my ski bag or on my desk at home?" His voice was gradually getting stronger. "I asked Frank to check my office here too and my locker. He said it wasn't in either place."

"Anu looked again and couldn't find it. Maybe it's in

your car? It's still parked at the mall," said Pat. "We checked all the pockets of your ski bag, but I didn't think to check the glove compartment, and I haven't had a chance to go back and get the car. They only just removed that damn boot."

"Oh, right. Maybe it's in there, or fell under my seat." Barry closed his eyes, took a deep breath, and then opened them again. "Susan, can you take Pat back to the mall to get the car?" He closed his eyes again.

"Of course," Susan said. "You won't be driving for a while." She looked over at his legs, both of which were in casts and suspended above the bed in slings. "But we'll at least get it back to your place and check a little more thoroughly for your phone." She patted his shoulder. "You should get some rest. We'll go do that and come back a bit later."

"Sounds good. I'm so tired." Barry's eyes closed again.

"Let's go," Susan whispered to Pat. "We can talk more in the car."

Pat nodded and accepted Susan's hand to help her stand, then grabbed her cane from the end of the bed.

Susan nodded with approval. The ortho had approved the removal of the boot as long as Pat was careful and used a cane. "Glad you're using that," she said and led her friend out of the hospital room.

"There's something really strange going on," Pat said as Susan put her keys into the ignition. "More than just a random break-in."

"I think you're right."

"Anu is really spooked and doesn't want to stay in the

house. She's staying with a friend, a massage girl from Thailand, I think. She manages a small salon in Satwa and lives in an apartment above it."

"I'm sure Anu's traumatized by the robbery." Susan took the exit onto Sheikh Zayed Road.

"No, it's more than that," Pat said. "She said she was looking for a file for Barry. He mentioned it in his delirium, remember?"

"Yes, I do recall that," Susan said. "What else did Anu say?"

"She said Barry told her it was marked 'research.' Then she didn't want to talk about it. She seems scared. And I'm sure it was her we saw at the hospital."

"I think so too," Susan agreed. "I didn't want to push the issue in case it made her clam up. She was pretty jumpy and kept looking out to the backyard while we were talking."

"I noticed that too," said Pat.

"I mean, it would be pretty terrifying, having two men barge into the house. I wonder if she's been able to give the police a description. And she's worried about Sara, her missing friend. Let's call her after we get Barry's car." Susan swore as a car sped up to her bumper and then swerved at the last minute into the right lane to pass her. "Jesus Christ, people drive like lunatics here." She took a deep breath and exhaled. "Are you going to be okay to drive with your ankle?"

"Yes, it's my left one, so I should be fine." Pat waved her hand, dismissing Susan's concerns. "It's not as awkward now without the boot. The ortho just said to be careful, take it slow. And, thank God it's the Audi and not his little sports car with the stick shift. My ankle still hurts if I put too much pressure on it, so I don't think I could do the clutch."

The two women fell silent as Susan concentrated on navigating the twelve lanes of speeding, tailgating vehicles, passing rows and rows of cement high-rises on both sides of the highway. She stayed as far to the right as she could without being in an exit lane. Changing lanes to make an exit was like driving in the Indy 500, with cars passing on both sides at great speeds. Preparing for an off-ramp had to be done strategically several exits in advance. If you missed an exit, it could take an hour or more to get back on track. It had happened to her when they first moved to Dubai, and it was an experience she didn't relish repeating.

They finally made it to the mall unscathed, and after a thorough search of Barry's car, determined his phone was not in it. They agreed to regroup back at Pat's to talk about what to do next.

Susan and Pat returned to the hospital with the hope that Barry was rested up and would remember something, anything, that would shed some light on the situation. As they exited the elevator and passed by the nurses' station, they heard a scream from the direction of Barry's room. Susan took to a sprint, almost knocking over the duty nurse as she hurried out from behind the desk.

Anu was sprawled on the floor just inside the door of Barry's room, holding her hand to her head, blood seeping through her headscarf and onto her fingers. There were bells going off on the machines and a staccato rhythm coming from the heart monitor. The nurse pushed past

Susan, barely looking at Anu lying on the floor as she rushed to Barry's bedside. Pat arrived just behind her.

"Code blue!" the nurse called out and pushed an emergency intercom on the wall. "He's in V-tach. No pulse. We need the crash cart." She started chest compressions.

"Move!" demanded Frank as he pushed into the room behind the team who wheeled in the cart. He grabbed the paddles. "Charge!" He waited for the beep. "Okay, clear." He placed them on Barry's chest and shocked him. Barry's body shuddered. Frank paused. "Charge again. Clear!" He laid the paddles on Barry's chest and shocked him again.

There was a reassuring blip, and Barry's heart regained its natural rhythm.

Pat stood paralyzed, watching from the corner of the room, while Susan helped Anu sit up. "Don't try to stand," Susan said quietly. She gently unwrapped Anu's scarf and winced at the sight of so much blood. She swallowed the bile that rose in her throat, bunched up the scarf, and held it to Anu's head, applying pressure to the wound.

All eyes in the room turned to them.

"What the hell happened?" Dr. Pettigrew snapped.

"I was just coming to see if Dr. Barry was okay." Anu choked on a sob.

Susan tightened her arm around Anu's shoulder. "It's okay. Just take a deep breath and tell us what happened."

Anu took a shaky breath and coughed. Then she winced.

"I think she's going to need stitches." Susan directed her comment to Frank. "And probably a CT scan."

"Is that right?" Frank growled. "First, she needs to tell us what she was doing here before I call the police."

"I didn't do anything!" Anu cried.

"Frank, she's our maid," said Pat, finally finding her

voice. "She's already traumatized by the break-in. Give her a chance to explain." Pat turned to her maid. "Anu, go on. What happened?"

"I opened the door and someone was standing over Dr. Barry with a pillow over his face. When they saw me, they ran and push me down. I scream and hit my head."

Dr. Pettigrew knelt down next to Anu and lifted the scarf Susan was holding to her wound. "Hmm. And what did the person look like? Did you get a good look?"

"I was so scared . . . it happened quick." Anu sniffed. "At first I think it's a lady. She . . . I thought it was she . . . was wearing abaya and shayla. You know, long black coat and headscarf."

"But you're not sure it was a woman?" Pat asked.

"No, Madame." Anu shook her head slowly. "It was a man. He was big and when he turned around and ran by, I can see his face too." She started crying.

"Nurse, bring a wheelchair for the young lady," Dr. Pettigrew said and stood up. "And ask one of the ER residents to clean up that cut and get some sutures in." He turned to Pat. "We need to call the police and make a report. And have security check the building." He sighed. "I'm sure he's long gone, but we have to follow protocol."

"Will Barry be okay?" Pat was back at her husband's side, holding his hand.

"He should be fine, but we'll have to watch him closely," Frank replied. "We're not sure how long his brain was deprived of oxygen. Hopefully your maid arrived before it was too long."

"What in God's name is going on, Frank? How do we know this maniac won't try again?"

Dr. Pettigrew put his hand on Pat's shoulder. "I will ask to have a security guard positioned outside Barry's door around the clock. We'll make sure he's safe. Once we make a police report, they will probably assign a detail to the hospital as well. They will want to question Anu, especially since she saw his face."

"Yes, of course . . . I . . ." Pat paused and let out a ragged breath. "I'm not leaving until we know what the hell's going on." She pulled the visitor's chair up to the bed and sat down. "You might as well bring the cot back in."

Frank nodded and left the room. The nurse, who had returned with a wheelchair, followed closely behind him, pushing Anu, who was holding her bloody scarf to her head.

Not ten minutes later, a security guard pulled up a chair outside Barry's door and settled himself on watch, arms crossed. He was a broad-shouldered young man with a menacing scowl.

"Well, that's reassuring," Susan said, closing the door. "He doesn't look like he's about to take any shit from anyone." She chuckled, then closed the door so he couldn't hear them.

"This isn't funny, Susan," Pat said. "Someone tried to kill Barry."

"I'm sorry, I know it's not. It's a bad habit. I laugh in uncomfortable situations. It's a defense mechanism, I guess."

"It's okay, but now I'm really scared." Pat let out a trembling sigh. "What if it wasn't an accident—the chairlift breaking, I mean—and someone came back to finish the job?"

"Now, don't jump to conclusions," said Susan.

"I think it's a logical one. First the 'accident,' then the break-in, and now this. There's definitely something going on."

"Let's not get ahead of ourselves. We need more information. At least now there's a guard at the door. Amazing that happened so quickly." Susan opened the door a crack and peeked out at the guard. "Yup, still there. If you're okay staying here by yourself, I'm going to go find Anu and see if she can shed any light on this bizarre situation, ask why she was here and how she thought Barry could help with her friend Sara. I'm sure the police are investigating the chairlift accident, so maybe we can call them and see if they found anything suspicious. And also ask whether they have any leads on the break-in."

"Okay, I'll be fine. Please text me later with an update. I'm not going anywhere." Pat turned back to her husband.

"I figured as much." Susan pulled the door open. "I'll keep you posted."

Pat nodded and waved her off.

CHAPTER
NINE

The hospital corridors were such a maze of glaringly white, identical hallways, Susan wondered how they kept people from "wandering around." Every hallway looked the same, but at least they had good signage to let you know what department you were inadvertently wandering through. She didn't intend to wander, she just wanted to find Anu. She had checked in the ER but there was no sign of her. She decided to check at Admitting on the main level near the entrance. She had passed it several times over the previous few days and recognized the man at the desk. At the private hospitals in Dubai, like this one, those who greeted visitors were given the same job title as those at a five-star hotel. She approached the desk and smiled at the concierge.

"I'm looking for a friend who was just brought down to have stitches in her head. She had a fall while visiting someone on the surgical floor, and I'm not sure where they took her. Her name is Anu."

"Let me check," he said and turned to his computer.

67

"Ah, here it is. Anu Kumara. Looks like they took care of her in the outpatient clinic. She's been released."

"When? I thought they were doing a CT scan." She also thought Anu would be held for questioning by police as an eyewitness to an attempted murder. The hospital should be on lockdown—there was a murderer on the loose. Susan would never understand why situations here were handled so differently.

The concierge looked at his computer. "Says here about ten minutes ago."

"Okay, thank you."

Susan ran out of the hospital and caught sight of Anu heading down the sidewalk. "Anu, wait!" she called.

The girl glanced over her shoulder and started walking faster, then broke into a run. Susan ran after her.

"Anu, I just want to help! Please stop."

Susan was gaining on her, and when Anu stopped and bent over with her hands on her knees, she almost ran into her. Anu wobbled and Susan caught her by the shoulders just in time to keep her from falling.

"I think I'm going to be sick," Anu mumbled.

"It's okay, I've got you." Susan guided her to a bench. The girl was so slightly built, her shoulders so narrow, that Susan almost encircled her with one arm. "You've had quite a knock on the head. I'm surprised they released you."

"It's a private hospital," Anu said. "The Thorntons pay for my health insurance, but it doesn't cover treatment here."

"But you hurt yourself here." Susan clicked her tongue. "And I thought the police would want to talk to you."

Anu started to cry. "I didn't mean to cause Dr. Barry and Ma'am Pat any trouble." She wiped a hand across her face.

"I just wanted help to find my friend. I don't want to make trouble."

Susan patted her knee. "Don't worry. You're not causing any trouble. And I'm going to help you find your friend." She handed Anu a tissue. "But you have to trust me. Maybe we could start by talking to some of your friends about those horrible stories of maids going missing."

"Not stories. It's true," Anu whispered and her eyes darted around. "The man who tried to hurt Dr. Barry . . . maybe he's still here?" Anu stood up. "I have to go!"

"Okay, but I'm coming with you." Susan stood and reached for her hand. "You shouldn't be alone right now, in case you have a concussion. You should really be lying down. I can take you home."

Anu shook her head. "No, not home. I will stay with my friend Jan, who works in massage parlor."

"Okay, I'll take you there, and once you have a rest, maybe we can talk to your friends together."

Susan knew Mitch would be angry with her for getting involved even more, but she didn't care. She'd get to the bottom of this one way or another, whether or not she stepped on anybody's toes or pissed someone off. Someone had tried to kill Barry, and she had a hunch it had something to do with Anu's missing friend.

When Susan and Anu arrived at the massage parlor, Jan was still working but gave them a key to let themselves into the apartment upstairs. Susan rummaged around in the bathroom cabinets and found some gauze and tape in a first aid kit. She checked Anu's stitches, changed the bandage, and encouraged her to have a rest. While the girl slept,

Susan sent an update to Pat and then a text to Mitch to let him know she wouldn't be home for supper. *He can cook his own dinner for a change!* she thought as she pressed send.

When Anu woke up two hours later, they made a plan to meet up with three of her friends at a playground in a compound in Al Sufouh, where one of them worked. The playground was under an overpass for Sheikh Zayed Road. The girls were fellow maids and nannies whom Anu had met through the hiring agency. They had kept in touch and would meet up on their rare mutual days off. Anu had shared with Susan that they often had picnics on the beach or went to the movies, but no matter what they were doing, they always shared stories and gossiped about the families who employed them. Anu had been embarrassed to admit that but swore she had never broken any confidences of the Thorntons. According to Anu, some of the other families were not nearly as nice as Barry and Pat.

When Susan asked, Anu said she and her friends rarely saw the girls who worked for local families, unless they caught sight of them briefly in one of the fashion malls. The nannies would be watching their charges while the Emirati mothers shopped or ate in the food courts. But stories swirled around about what it was like to work behind those very tall cement walls that surrounded most homes, some with barbed wire at the top. For the most part, the maids and nannies were treated well, but there were some employers who confiscated the passports of helpers when they arrived and made them work on demand, around the clock with no days off and only one or two weeks off a year. Susan had heard the stories but had ignored them because she thought they were dramatic exaggerations.

As she and Anu approached the playground, Susan saw three young women sitting side by side on the bench closest to the path. One girl wound and unwound a hankie around her fingers, while another twisted her braid that hung over one shoulder. The third one kept looking over her shoulder and then at the three children playing on the swings, who ranged in age from about four to eight. Susan assumed she was the one who worked in the compound.

"Ma'am Susan, these are my friends, May, Hana, and Mira."

All three young women gave furtive glances at Susan, then cast their eyes down.

Susan reached out her hand. "Hello, May, it's so nice to meet you."

May put her hankie on her lap and accepted the hand that was offered. Susan smiled and turned to the girl with the long braid.

"And you're Hana?" The girl nodded and shook Susan's hand. "Nice to meet you too. And Mira? What a pretty name," Susan said.

She felt a twinge in her heart for these girls. Having worked with many fragile people in her nursing career, she quickly saw the signs of abuse or at least fear of saying or doing the wrong thing. Job security was tenuous for any expat but especially so for these girls.

It came naturally to Susan to put people at ease. The bench was full, so she lowered herself to the ground and sat cross-legged in front of them. "Thank you so much for being here," she began. "Anu told me you are worried about some of your friends."

They all nodded.

"Well, I'd like to help you find out what happened to them, if that's okay."

"Mira, watch me!"

Susan turned to see a little girl pumping her legs to

make the swing go higher as her brother pushed from behind. The third child, who appeared to be a little sister, played quietly in a sandbox off to the side.

"I see you!" Mira called back. "Not too high, okay?"

"Okay!" the little girl called back and giggled.

"They look like they're very happy," Susan said to Mira. "You must be doing a good job."

"Thank you, ma'am."

"Please, call me Susan." She looked to each of them, ensuring eye contact. "I'd like to hear why you're worried and what you've seen or heard."

"You can tell Ma'am Susan," Anu assured them. "She wants to help."

Mira was the first to share. "My friend was nanny for the children right next door to me." She paused and swallowed as tears welled up in her eyes. Susan handed Mira a tissue and waited, not wanting her to feel any pressure. Mira wiped her eyes and continued. "On a day off, about a month ago, we went to the beach and she told me she was pregnant. But then she got scared and ran off before she told me anything else. I did not see her ever since."

"Oh, Mira," Susan said. "That must be so worrisome for you. Maybe we can look into it and find her, make sure she's okay." Susan reached for her hand and gave it a squeeze.

"That's Sara, I tell you about her already," Anu added. "She's my friend too, and I ask Dr. Barry to help find . . ." Her voice trailed off and she looked down at her hands folded on her lap.

More stories spilled out as the girls warmed up to Susan. Hana and Mira shared one story after another of girls they either knew personally or who were friends of friends who were sent home, and some who, they claimed, never made it home.

Susan sat quietly and listened, mostly because she was dumbfounded and didn't know what to say. She realized the problem was huge. Through the whole story-sharing, May sat, hands folded on her lap, clutching her hankie, saying nothing.

"May, is there someone you know who has gone missing or has told you she's in trouble?" Susan asked.

"Um . . . uh, no, ma'am," May stuttered. "I know same girls Hana and Mira do. No more."

"It's okay, May. Anu?"

"One of my friends, Kan, was a massage girl from Thailand," said Anu. "She did home visits and sometimes came for Ma'am Pat and Dr. Barry. She told me a couple months ago about a client who make her very uncomfortable, a high-level government man who forced her to do things she didn't want." The girls nodded. "I ask Ma'am Pat if she know anyone who wants a maid or nanny. My friend doesn't want to be massage girl anymore. Ma'am Pat, she tell me about a friend name Nala who needed a nanny."

"Do you mean Nala Al Qasimi?"

"Yes, Ma'am Pat's friend," Anu said. She shifted on the bench and tugged on her headscarf.

Pat had introduced Susan to Nala at one of the EWG committee meetings. Susan already knew her by reputation as someone who had helped the EWG with charity fundraisers. Nala had connections and she drew in other local women to support the causes of the group.

It was unusual for Thai women to work as maids or nannies in Dubai, but if Anu's friend had originally come to Dubai to work at a massage parlor and had been lured under false pretenses, then it would be like Nala to help the girl out.

"We were all supposed to meet at the mall last week.

Kan never come. And she never answered our messages. That's when I told Dr. Barry about my friends, about Sara and Kan. I thought he would help because he know Kan." Anu chewed her lip. "It happen many times. Now I have to say something."

"Well, I'm glad you're all speaking up now," began Susan, "but if your employers knew you were talking to me it could be dangerous for you. We don't know exactly why your friends have disappeared and who is involved. So please don't say anything to anyone else. Let me take it from here. And be careful. Watch out for each other. I think we should exchange numbers, stay in touch."

The girls were visibly relieved, and after sharing their numbers, May and Hana got up to leave. They all hugged goodbye.

"I have to get the children inside for supper," said Mira. She called to the kids on the playground and waved to Anu and Susan. "Thank you, ma'am, for helping." She scurried away, shooing the children as she went.

"Anu, can you take me to Nala's, where Kan was working?"

"I don't think so, ma'am." Anu looked down at her hands.

"Do you know where it is?"

"Yes, ma'am, but . . ."

"Anu, Nala may be able to tell us where Kan is. It may lead us to Sara too. It's important I speak with her."

Anu looked up as tears filled her eyes. "Okay, I will take you," she said, her voice cracking. "It's very close."

Susan gave her a hug. "Let's go then."

~

Susan pressed the ringer on the gate of a large mansion on Al Wasl Road. As she and Anu waited for a reply, Susan wondered if it was such a good idea to show up unannounced. Before she could change her mind, a speaker outside the gate crackled.

"Yes, can I help you?"

"Um, we're here to see Nala . . . Mrs. Al Qasimi?"

"May I tell her who is here to see her and what is your purpose?"

"My name is Susan Morris, I'm a member of EWG. I wanted to talk to her about our upcoming fundraiser."

Anu looked at her, puzzled. Susan shrugged her shoulders. She thought Nala probably wouldn't invite them in if she said she was looking for information on missing maids.

"I can't be here," Anu whispered. "Here comes the bus. I will go to Jan's." She abruptly turned and was dashing to the bus stop across the street when the voice came through the speaker again.

"Please come in, Mrs. Al Qasimi will see you."

The loud buzz allowing her entry further jangled Susan's nerves. She pulled on the handle before the buzzing stopped, then turned and saw the bus pull away. Anu was no longer on the sidewalk. Susan shook her head, pulled the gate open wider, and stepped into an expansive courtyard. She would check in on Anu later.

A woman who Susan assumed was Nala's maid waved at her from a massive front door beckoning her to come. Susan crossed the courtyard and walked up three steps that led to a stunning foyer with huge bouquets of fresh flowers in every corner and a rich red-and-gold Persian silk rug, at least twenty by twenty feet, that practically covered the entire floor of the entryway.

Susan was taking it all in, trying not to let her jaw drop,

when Nala floated onto the scene. Her colorful silk caftan flowed in diaphanous wisps around her, giving her a movie star look. Susan thought that she likely hadn't put on a head covering as her visitor was female. When she had seen Nala at various committee meetings and luncheons, she was always wearing the traditional black abaya and hijab that most Emirati women wore in public. Hers were very stylish with colorful trim around the sleeves and down the front. She always carried the latest Gucci bag and wore shoes with red soles. Susan didn't really follow fashion but knew that red-soled shoes were all the rage. She suddenly felt desperately underdressed, even for a one-on-one home visit. She ran her hand down her khaki-covered thighs. She realized she must look a mess having sat in the dusty wind at the playground for the past hour or so. Her curly mop was unruly at the best of times; she wished she had tied it back. She had considered getting it all cut off, but Mitch told her that with short hair she looked like one of the Jonas brothers, only not as tall.

"What a lovely surprise," Nala said and put her hand out. "Susan, isn't it?"

Susan thought she heard a hint of sarcasm that indicated her showing up out of the blue wasn't as "lovely" as all that.

"Yes, hello, Nala." She shook the offered hand. "I'm sorry to show up unannounced. I hope I'm not interrupting your dinner."

"Oh no, we tend to eat late. My husband isn't even home from work yet." Nala put her hand on the small of Susan's back. "Let's sit where it's comfortable." She turned to her maid. "Can you please bring us some cold juice and biscuits, Isa? Thank you."

Susan knew Nala's husband was a minister in the upper

echelons of the Dubai government, but she wasn't sure what role he played. She also knew that Nala didn't work per se but was a stay-at-home mom—with lots of help, it seemed—who did charity work on a very visible level.

Nala led Susan into an exquisitely decorated living room. Once they were seated, she said, "So, what can I help you with? You said it had something to do with the EWG fundraiser? I just spoke with Pat yesterday. Awful thing, her husband's accident and then her home being broken into like that. It's so rare in Dubai. I assured her that we would find other items to replace what was stolen and that she should just be with her husband and not worry about it."

"Oh, yes, Pat asked me to follow up with you." Susan grabbed onto the olive branch being extended, even if it wasn't entirely true. "She is spending all her time at the hospital with Barry." Susan accepted the glass of juice presented to her by Nala's maid who had quietly entered the living room. "Thank you." Susan set the glass on the large glass and marble coffee table in front of her. "Um, there is something else I wanted to ask you about though."

"Oh? And, what is that?"

"It's a sensitive issue, one I'm hoping you can help me with." Susan shifted in her chair and leaned forward. "Pat's maid, Anu, said a friend of hers, Kan, was working for you." Susan paused, wondering how Nala would react to the change of topic.

"Yes, I hired Kan to be my nanny. She had been a massage therapist but didn't want to do that anymore." Nala straightened the books on her coffee table. Her hand paused on the glossy cover of *Shimmering Skyscrapers: A Photographic Journey Through Dubai*. "She had come here a few times to do some reflexology on my feet. She had several certifications and was very good."

"Anu said she was pregnant," Susan said.

Nala raised her eyebrows and sighed. "Yes, she was, and I offered to help her. I told her she could work here until the time came and she could have the baby here. Kan had confided in me that she had been abused by one of her clients." Nala shook her head. "At first, I didn't tell my husband she was pregnant. Initially she agreed to stay on. But she decided she wanted to go home. I—" Nala started as a car door slammed. "That is my husband. He'll be wanting his supper." She looked nervously toward the foyer.

"Anu and her friends were supposed to meet with Kan at the mall a week or so ago and she didn't show up. They also told me that they have heard of pregnant maids and nannies going missing. I know it's against the law to have sex out of wedlock here, but as I understand it, these girls were raped."

"Nala, I'm home," a male voice called.

"I'm in here, darling," Nala called back and turned to Susan. "I'm sorry, you have to go. All I know is that we bought Kan a ticket to Bangkok, and she left last week. I know she got home okay because she sent me a text when she landed." Nala pulled out her phone and scrolled through the texts then turned the screen toward Susan.

"Well, that's good news," Susan said. "I know Anu will be relieved." She stood up to leave. "Do you have an address for Kan in Bangkok? My husband will be traveling there in the next few days. He's a pilot and I often go on layovers with him. Perhaps I can go and see if she's okay."

"Ma'am Nala?" The maid hovered in the entrance to the living room. "Mister has gone to his rooms to change and will meet you for dinner in fifteen minutes. I told him you had a visitor."

"Okay, thank you, Isa, I'll be right there. If you could get the children ready, that would be helpful. They're upstairs in the playroom watching cartoons." She turned back to Susan. "All I know is she planned to move back in with her family. They own a restaurant in Patpong—Sawadee Café—and live above it. Not the best place to raise a child . . ." Nala's voice trailed off.

"You've been so helpful, thank you." Susan took Nala's hand and squeezed it.

"You're welcome. I hope Kan is okay. Do let me know if you talk to her."

"I will." Susan turned and followed Isa, who escorted her out to the courtyard.

Anu got off the bus a few stops past Nala's in front of the Choithrams grocery store. She stood at the curb watching for a break in traffic and could see May crouched next to the entrance waiting for her.

"I got your text on the bus," Anu said, catching her breath after her dash across the street. "What do you need to talk to me about? Are you okay?" She knelt next to her friend who had started crying.

"Oh, Anu," May began, "I don't know what to do . . ."

Anu took her hand. "About what?" She had a sinking feeling in the pit of her stomach.

"I'm pregnant," May whispered and dissolved into a fresh flood of tears.

The house sat in darkness. Even the outside light was not turned on. Susan put the Jeep in park and took a deep breath to gather her wits about her. She knew what she had to do but also knew it would take some convincing for Mitch to agree. Maybe she wouldn't share all the details. She knew he was annoyed by her "meddling," but she felt strongly that it wasn't meddling. She was helping out friends who desperately needed it. Living in a foreign country was hard enough on a day-to-day basis, let alone when something unexpected happened, which it did frequently. That's why friendships developed quickly among expats; people didn't have family close by to count on.

Since moving to Dubai, Susan often felt that as soon as she had things figured out, another curveball would come at her. Anything ranging from what documents were required to renew residence visas to how to get the Internet hooked up. The paperwork was overwhelming for things that were so simple back home. Throw in a hospitalization or any situation that involved law enforcement, and everything could go quickly off the rails. As expats, they had very few rights, unless your company went to bat for you. Susan knew they were lucky that way. EmAir was a powerful, well-respected, government-owned, and well-connected company that smoothed the way for their employees for most processes when they were first getting settled. Now there were things Susan had to maneuver on her own, especially when Mitch was away. But there were things she couldn't do without her husband, as she found out when she called the bank one day and was told they could only release account information to Mitch, even though Susan was sure it was a joint account. These instances were a constant source of irritation. Although when she thought about it, she wondered if that was the way Mitch had set up their account. She would have to ask him about that. He had been a bit cagey lately about sharing banking information. She hadn't felt it necessary to push it, but something didn't feel right. However, she had other things to worry about just now.

She let herself into the darkened entryway, turned on the light just inside the door, and flipped the switch for the porch light as well. She kicked off her shoes and padded quietly down the hallway toward the bedroom. A light was coming from under the closed door of the office at the end of the hall. Susan hadn't expected Mitch to be home.

She said his name as she opened the door. "Mitch?"

He closed his laptop and swiveled his chair around.

"Hey, you're home," he said and stood up. He reached for her. She almost stepped back but rethought her approach. She was still pissed at him, but she had to put that aside. She needed his help.

"Yes, it's been a day!" She walked toward him and felt the familiar comfort of his arms as they wrapped around her. Maybe everything was okay. Could she have overreacted? Mitch tended to forget their squabbles quicker than she did, but she still couldn't bring herself to forgive and forget this latest one. She didn't believe his story about where the condoms came from, but she would save that for another time. "Did you eat?" As she said the words her stomach grumbled.

"Yeah, I did, but it sounds like you didn't." He chuckled and released her from his embrace. "I got your message so I went out and had a bite with Tom at the pub in the compound next door. I have a leftover falafel if you want it. They give you two humongous ones, and I could only eat one."

"I love their falafels," said Susan. "I need to go to the bathroom first." She headed into the en suite. "Keep me company while I'm eating? Have a glass of wine with me," she called over her shoulder.

"I've already got a beer going, but I will join you," Mitch replied.

A few minutes later they settled into the breakfast nook in the corner of the kitchen. Mitch poured Susan a glass of wine, and she took a bite of the falafel.

"Oh yum! It never disappoints."

They sat in silence while Susan ate and Mitch scrolled through his phone. Susan didn't know where to start, so rather than getting annoyed at being ignored, she took advantage of him being distracted. She swallowed the last bite and wiped her mouth with her napkin. She took her wine glass and leaned back in her chair. She cleared her throat.

"So, I noticed on your schedule you have a Bangkok trip

tomorrow." She hoped it sounded conversational, not leading anywhere.

"Yeah, I do," Mitch said and put his phone face down on the table.

"That'll be great, you've been there so many times now you won't have to study the flight plan and runway layout as much."

"Always good to do a refresher," said Mitch. "And we're constantly getting updates for the flight manuals. I have a bunch of pages I need to swap out. I think I even saw some for Suvarnabhumi, but I'll do that in the morning. Pickup is around eleven, so I'll have time."

"I love Bangkok," began Susan. "Every time we've gone, we only spend a day or two before we continue on to some island. I'd like to go again sometime."

"Yeah, it's an interesting city."

"Maybe I should go with you on your layover tomorrow."

"Oh, Suze, it's kind of late to be planning that. We don't even know if there's space on the flight," Mitch said. "Another time, okay?"

"Oh, come on, please? I need a change of scenery. Can you check now?"

"It's late and I really should get to bed."

"Mitch, you never go to bed before midnight when you don't have an early pickup." She leaned forward and put her hand on his. "Please? I know it's a short layover and you'll have to sleep most of the time, but I can amuse myself. It's so easy to get around."

"Jesus, you're not going to let this go, are you?" He shook his head. "Okay, let me look at the flight and see if there's a seat in business. It's the best chance you'll have to get a seat on standby."

"Excellent! Thanks, hon." Ignoring his exasperation, Susan picked up her plate and empty wine glass and went to the kitchen sink. "I'll wash up these few dishes while you check on that."

Her mind was a whir as she started to put a plan together to visit Kan in Patpong.

As Susan boarded the plane to Bangkok, she couldn't help but smile to herself. There had been plenty of empty seats in business class; Mitch had easily bought her a standby ticket, and now she had her boarding pass in hand.

The flight attendant at the entrance smiled at her as Susan showed her pass. The attendant was stunning with sleek black hair pulled tightly back into a bun at the nape of her neck. The word *statuesque* came to mind. The red pillbox hat she wore as part of the uniform had a swatch of gauzy beige material flowing down one side and wrapped around the neck. She wore the standard bright red lipstick that matched the hat and the high-heeled pumps. It was a red that Susan could never pull off on her lips. The most she ever wore was lip gloss with maybe a faint pink tint. Once the plane took off, the flight attendants would remove the hat and scarf and switch to smart flats to proceed with the world-class service EmAir was known for.

"Would I be able to speak with Captain Morris?" Susan asked the attendant.

"I'm sorry, ma'am, but the captain is busy doing the preflight check."

"Oh, sorry, of course he is," Susan said. "I'm his wife and I just wanted him to know I got on the flight."

"I will let him know." The attendant sounded annoyed

but then seemed to check herself and smiled, eyes narrowing. She turned to welcome the next passenger boarding, effectively dismissing her.

Susan made her way to her seat and proceeded to make herself comfortable. She opened the plastic wrapping containing a blanket and slippers and kicked off her shoes. She looked up as the same flight attendant approached.

"Captain Morris says he will meet you in the galley after takeoff."

"Okay, thank you."

The words weren't even out of Susan's mouth before the woman had turned to the passenger across the aisle to ask if she could get him a water, a juice, or a glass of champagne. She hadn't asked Susan if she wanted anything. Susan shrugged to herself. She would just as soon wait until they were at cruising altitude anyway. There would be plenty of time during the six-and-a-half-hour flight to take advantage of a glass or two of wine and a nice meal. She'd even watch a movie or two. She settled in and closed her eyes, semi-snoozing through the safety demonstration, taxi, and takeoff.

When she heard the ding that indicated they were allowed to unbuckle their seat belts and move around the cabin, she figured Mitch would be headed to the galley any minute. She tossed her blanket aside and slid her feet into the slippers. She knew he couldn't stay long. She made her way up the aisle and opened the curtain to the galley. Mitch was there talking and laughing with the flight attendant who had welcomed Susan aboard. They looked a bit too cozy for Susan's liking. She couldn't help but notice that the attendant was almost as tall as Mitch, even in her flats. Mitch turned to Susan as she pulled the curtain closed behind her.

She forced a smile, stood on tiptoes and tilted her chin up for a kiss. He turned his head and her lips grazed his cheek. He shook his head very slightly. *Oh, right. No public displays of affection.* Surely it was okay with no one around. Oh, except *her*. Susan glared just a little at the dark-haired beauty. *Lettie from Thailand* her name tag said.

"Well, I'm glad you got a seat," Mitch said. "I'm just going to pop into the bathroom, then I have to get back to the cockpit."

"Oh, okay," Susan replied. "Don't work too hard then, until it's time to land, that is." She laughed but neither Mitch nor Lettie did.

"Yeah, I'll try to get you safely on the ground."

She caught him rolling his eyes as he turned to Lettie and gave her one of his electric smiles. She beamed back at him then turned to her task of pouring champagne into flutes. She passed one to Susan and then practically shooed her out of the galley. Susan could feel her blood boiling as she made her way back to her seat, gripping her glass. She couldn't shake the feeling of jealousy, and she fumed thinking how rude they had both been to her. She would certainly bring it up with Mitch when they got to their hotel room.

The ride to the hotel on the crew bus was a lively one with all the flight attendants talking and making dinner plans. Susan sat in a back corner by a window. Mitch usually saved her a seat on the crew bus, but not this time. He was toward the front, practically holding court. If Susan didn't know him better, she would have called it flirting. But she was right here, on the bus. That would just be too blatant, wouldn't it? He didn't mean anything by it, did he?

Mitch and the first officer approached the counter in the hotel lobby, while all the flight attendants hung back. It was very different from Western flight crews. The EmAir pilots got their room keys first, and then the rest were allowed to check in. Susan marched up to the counter and stood beside Mitch, marking her territory. She knew it was childish but didn't care. He turned to her and nodded. Without saying a word, they both headed for the elevator.

The silence continued on the elevator ride to the eleventh floor and down the long hallway, decorated with red and gold lanterns hanging from the ceiling every ten feet or so. Normally, Susan would have stopped to admire the intricate patterns, even take pictures, but her anger powered her forward as she followed two steps behind her long-legged husband.

As the door clicked closed, Mitch spun around to face her. His face was flushed and she could see the muscles in his jaw twitching.

"What?" Susan asked, somewhat taken aback at his expression.

"I can't believe how rude you were to the flight attendants."

"Flight attendants, plural? Or just one? I think it was you and *Lettie* who were rude to me!" Her nostrils flared and green eyes flashed as waves of jealousy simmered under the surface.

"Don't be ridiculous." He lifted his suitcase onto the rack, put his flight bag on the desk, and took off his hat. "We were trying to work, and honestly, you were in the way."

Susan raised her eyebrows and sighed, her anger

doused, replaced by confusion. "I'm sorry it felt that way." She sat on the edge of the bed. "What's going on, Mitch? You've been so easily agitated lately and even cold at times. I don't get it."

Susan's phone pinged. She pulled it out of her pocket and gazed down at the message. "Oh shit!"

"What? Who's it from?" He walked over and sat down next to her.

"It's from Pat," Susan said. "The other day, I went to visit a . . . a friend, and Anu came with me. She left without me and got on the bus."

"So?"

"So . . . Pat says she never got to the friend's place where she's staying."

"Isn't she a live-in? Why would she be staying with a friend?"

"It's a long story."

"Does it have something to do with Barry's accident?"

Susan hesitated. "Um, sort of . . ."

"Aw, Suze, I told you not to get involved."

"Well, I am involved and that's that," Susan said. She shifted her position to face him. "Actually, it's why I wanted to come on layover with you."

"I don't like the sounds of this, Susan." Mitch stood up and paced to the window and back.

"Young women are going missing, Mitch, and I can't sit on my hands and do nothing." She looked at him, waiting for a response. When she didn't get one, she continued. "There's a gal here who got pregnant in Dubai; her family owns a restaurant in Patpong." Mitch opened his mouth to say something, but she continued quickly before he could interrupt. "She was raped by one of her clients, and Nala, the friend I went to see, sort of snuck her out of the country."

He put his hands over his ears. "Don't say any more. This is crazy and I don't want to know what you're up to. I want to have . . . what's it called? Plausible deniability. Susan, I could lose my job."

"Mitch, I don't think your job is more important than the lives of these women!"

"What about our lives? You don't know how high up this goes. If the police or anyone finds out you're digging around where you shouldn't be, you could be thrown in jail."

"Now, that's crazy. I'm not doing anything wrong."

"That's a matter of perspective, Susan." He sat down beside her and took her hand. "We're living in a foreign country. Things are different, you know that." He shook his head. "You almost got killed in Saudi when you rushed off half-cocked with Celeste to find Tamara. Didn't you learn your lesson? Please, don't do anything stupid, like going to see this girl."

"What lesson? We found Tamara and that's what's important. I'm sorry, but I have to find Kan, make sure she's okay. She hasn't been responding to texts from her friends, and they're really worried." Susan stood up and tossed her suitcase on the second queen bed in the room, unzipped it, and pulled out her cosmetic bag. "I'm going to freshen up and then head out. You can come with me or not." She walked into the bathroom and closed the door, leaned her back on it, and let out the breath she was holding.

The bright lights and pounding disco music swirled around her as she walked the main drag of Soi Patpong, Bangkok's infamous red-light district. It got Susan's adrenaline pumping, not because it felt dangerous but because it felt forbidden. She had never experienced anything like it anywhere else in the world. She had only been there once before, but in the daylight and with Mitch. He had chosen not to accompany her this time as he needed to get some sleep. It was a short tram ride from the hotel, and Susan felt safe enough. It was early evening and the real debauchery wouldn't start for a while yet. She would be back to the hotel long before that.

She had looked up the address of the Sawadee Café, but it was hard to find a number on any of the bars, discos, and restaurants. One blended into another, making it difficult to see where one ended and another began. She felt a hand on her elbow.

"Sawadee ka," said the smiling woman holding her arm. "Free show for you, Madame? Come see Ping-Pong show."

Susan squinted and wondered if it was a transgender woman—in Thailand, they were known as ladyboys—standing beside her, stroking her arm. "Oh, no thank you," she said, pulling her elbow from the woman's grip. Susan had heard about these shows, knew women would shoot Ping-Pong balls out of their vaginas, something Susan had no desire to see. She was on a mission to find Kan's family's restaurant. "Maybe you can help me?"

"Oh yes, Madame, we have great show and many drinks," the woman said. "Come see." She started to guide Susan into the go-go bar.

"No, no, I'm looking for a particular place. Where is

number two-eight-five? It's called Sawadee Café. Is it close?"

"Ah, Madame, over that way." She pointed. "Almost to end. It's restaurant, not bar. Here we have Ping-Pong show. You like better."

"No, thank you." Susan backed away. "Maybe another time. Thank you for your help."

Susan hurried away before her elbow was grabbed again or her rear end was stroked. There was a lot of grabbing and prodding going on, and it was making her feel uncomfortable. It was a relief to know that Kan's family owned a restaurant, not one of the bars touting sex shows. All it took was a quick glance into any of the open doors and you could see young Thai women—or ladyboys, it was hard to tell—in various stages of undress, undulating and swinging around poles sprouting from the bar tops.

When she was almost to the end of Soi Patpong, Susan caught sight of the restaurant sign right on the corner of Si Lom Road and jogged the rest of the way. She kicked off her shoes outside the door and stepped inside the air-conditioned restaurant. It was busy, with almost all of the booths occupied. A young woman approached her.

"Hello, may I help you?"

"Yes, I'm looking for Kan. Is she here?"

"I am Kan." The girl narrowed her eyes at Susan. "Who are you?"

"I'm a friend of Nala's."

The girl backed away. Tears welled in her eyes.

"And Anu's." Susan smiled, trying to reassure the girl she was a friend. "They want to know you're okay. They've been trying to reach you."

"I don't want to talk to you." She turned and walked toward the back of the restaurant.

"Please, I want to help. I hear you're pregnant."

The girl spun around. "There's no more baby," she whispered and looked around, putting her finger to her lips. "Shh!" She wiped her hand over her eyes. "It's gone."

Susan lowered her voice. "I'm not sure what you mean."

"Come," Kan said, then called to another woman and said something in Thai. She took Susan's hand and led her to a back corner and slid into the last empty booth, motioning for Susan to sit on the other side. She took a deep breath and told Susan her story.

Susan's head was spinning as she rode the tram back to the hotel. What Kan had told her was so shocking it was hard to process. Kan confirmed that Nala had been supportive and tried to protect her. Nala's husband knew about the baby, and Nala had suggested they let Kan stay and quietly have her baby, but he had refused. He did agree to buy her a ticket home and let her leave without informing the authorities that she was pregnant. He even arranged to have her taken to the airport. What Susan hoped Nala didn't know was that Kan had been taken to the hospital first where she was forced to end the pregnancy "for her own good," right then and there. After all, the child had been conceived out of wedlock. The fact that it was the result of a rape went unacknowledged. When Kan had gone through immigration at the airport, the day after her abortion, they stamped her visa *terminated*, and she was escorted to the plane. She was told never to come back or she would be arrested for having sexual relations outside of marriage and for aborting her pregnancy, both of which were illegal.

Susan wasn't sure what to do with the information but was anxious to get home and see Pat and find Anu. She had hoped that after meeting with Kan, she would be armed with more evidence to take to the police, but now she wasn't sure what to do. Nala and her husband were very well-connected, and it wasn't clear if either of them knew about Kan's forced abortion. Susan would have to tread very lightly.

As Susan waited in the immigration line to reenter the UAE, she watched Mitch and the other pilot and flight attendants head to the crew line. Her nerves stood on end as she inched forward in line. When she finally got to the front, she handed the immigration officer her passport. He scanned it and read the screen, then looked up at her. He waved to a supervisor behind him who stepped forward and looked over the officer's shoulder at the screen. He took Susan's passport.

"Follow me," he said.

"Okay. May I ask why?" Susan had to speed-walk in order to keep up with the man's long stride.

"Sit here," he said and pointed to a row of chairs outside a door that said *Visas* on it. "We need to check your residence visa."

"It should be fine for another year," Susan said. "I've just had it renewed. My husband is a pilot. He's here in the airport."

"Sit." The man pointed to the chair again and disappeared into the office, closing the door with a solid *thunk.*

Susan could see Mitch heading toward the exit in animated conversation with Lettie. They were passing right by, and she waved frantically to catch his attention. Mitch looked over and raised his eyebrows. She shrugged. He turned and waved at his crew and walked over to where Susan was sitting.

"What's up? Why are you still here? I thought you'd already be in a cab on your way home."

"I'm not sure. They said they're checking my visa."

"It's probably just a spot check," Mitch said. "It'll be fine." He patted her shoulder. "I have to go upstairs and close out the flight plan. It shouldn't take long. I'll cancel the crew driver and meet you at the taxi stand out front."

"If you don't see me, please come back. Something doesn't feel right."

"I'm sure it's fine," Mitch said. "See you shortly."

Susan sighed, took her phone out and texted Pat to let her know she was back in Dubai and she'd fill her in when she saw her. She looked up as the door opened and an officer came out. He walked past her and into the arrivals hall. It felt like an eternity before the door finally opened again and two officers came out and stood in front of her. They spoke in Arabic and motioned for her to follow them into the room. The door closed behind them and they pointed toward another row of seats. Susan sat down.

"Can I ask what the problem is?"

One of the officers shook his head. "We'll be back."

Another several agony-filled minutes went by, and then the door opened again. One of the officers came back in, followed closely by Mitch. She looked at him, puzzled.

"Susan, what the hell? They think you were traveling on a pass for work. You know that's against the rules. I've tried to explain that you're not working here and you had just come on a layover with me. What did you tell the guy when you gave him your passport?"

"Nothing! He didn't ask me anything. Just handed my passport to the supervisor, and then I was brought here."

"Well, they say you can come home with me, but they're going to hold on to your passport for now."

"What? Why?"

"I'm not sure but we can't argue with them. Let's go home. I'll call HR tomorrow and they can work on getting it back."

He stormed out the door and Susan followed quickly behind.

CHAPTER
ELEVEN

Mitch snapped his bag shut and swung it off the bed. He strode into the walk-in closet and yanked a jacket off a hanger. It had been a full twenty-four hours since the Bangkok trip, and he had finally calmed down a bit.

"Try to stay out of trouble while I'm gone." He walked over to Susan sitting on the edge of the bed and kissed her on the head.

Susan hated when he did that. It was so patronizing. He only did it when she wasn't doing what he wanted her to do. She pulled away from him and stood up and glared at him. She had to tilt her head back, and her chin jutted out.

"That's not fair," she said. "I haven't done anything wrong."

Mitch let out a long breath and shook his head. "As I said before, Suze, that's a matter of opinion. The laws are different here, you know that." He sighed. "I really wish you could come with me. I know Mom and Dad and Stan would love to see you."

"I'd love to see them too, but I can't travel anywhere until they give me my passport back."

"I know. I don't know what the holdup is, but I'm told HR is on it and it will be returned. They know I'll be away for a week or so. They'll put it in my mail file at work. I'll get it when I get back."

It pissed Susan off that her husband would be sent her passport, not her, but at the same time she was almost relieved that she didn't have it. Gave her an excuse not to go with Mitch to New Jersey. He had to go to sign paperwork to take over the power of attorney for his brother. His parents had insisted they could still handle all the logistics of his care, but his mother had had a fall and was in the hospital. Mitch had finally put his foot down, and they agreed power of attorney should go to him. As an airline employee he was lucky to be able to travel at the last minute. His family, including Susan, could too. It was useful in situations like this.

New Jersey held too many bad memories for Susan, albeit some good ones too. Susan and Mitch had left New Jersey after the lawsuit with her patient's family had been dropped, and they had spent a brief time in North Carolina before moving to Dubai. With both her parents gone, Mitch's family was the only reason for her to go back to New Jersey, other than to visit a few friends from high school who still lived there. But they all had busy jobs and kids, and she didn't have much in common with them anymore.

Mitch's absence would be a good opportunity to figure out where Anu had gone and to fill Pat in on the details of her visit with Kan. Susan had taken the day yesterday to regroup, recover from a bit of jet lag, and catch up on laundry, but she knew she couldn't hold off telling Pat about her trip much longer. As for Nala, Susan hadn't decided whether or not to update her. It had occurred to her that Nala's husband, or even Nala herself, could be involved somehow in the whole mess. Susan didn't know whom she could trust, and she knew she had to be careful.

"It's going to be a tough visit without you," Mitch said, breaking into Susan's thoughts. "You've always been the one best able to soothe Stan. I'll never forget the day we met. He was having one of his migraines, and you were cradling his head on your lap, talking to him in soothing tones. It was obvious what you were doing was helping the pain go away. You have healing hands." Mitch's eyes started to well up.

When it came to Stan, Mitch was a big softy. The only time she ever saw him cry was when he was talking about his brother. Stan had been diagnosed with schizophrenia in his mid-twenties, and eventually the severity of his symptoms meant he had to be cared for 24-7.

Susan gave Mitch a hug. "I'm sure he has other nurses and caregivers he's bonded with." She didn't want to discuss her nursing career. She wasn't going back to it. She hated the sight of blood, which was why she had chosen psychiatric nursing. But, as an empath, she absorbed her patients' mental and physical hurts and got way too attached.

"I suppose so," Mitch said and wiped his eyes. "I'd better get going. I think my taxi's here. I heard a car horn."

Susan walked him to the door and opened it. "Tell your folks and Stan I promise I'll see them at Christmas."

"Okay, will do." He bent down and gave her a peck on the cheek and walked out, closing the door behind him.

She stood in the living room window and watched the taxi pull away, gave a wave, and then let the curtain fall back into place. She headed into the office and sat down at the computer to google Nala's husband. She wanted to see just how far up in the government he was and what department he worked in.

She switched on the computer and the screen that came up was open to Mitch's email. *That's strange.* He usually logged off his email when he was going out of town. Then her blood ran cold. She squinted at the sender's name on the last incoming message, not believing what she was seeing—Lettie! Her hand inadvertently clicked on open. She would never read Mitch's email, ever. Until now.

Lettie's reply read:

I'm sorry too! Next time . . . miss you.

ooxoxo

Susan's heart started thumping against her chest wall. She thought it might actually break through and shatter her breastbone. She slowly scrolled down to read Mitch's original message.

Hello sweetheart,

I'm so sorry that Susan came on our layover. Kind of put a damper on our plans, didn't it? I promise I'll make it up to you.

It was followed by several hearts and kissy-face emojis.

A sob escaped Susan's lips. She sat back in the chair as a wave of desolation and hurt overtook her. The tears flowed and her body vibrated with every sob. *How could he?* A haze of confusion infiltrated the synapses of her brain. She cried for what felt like hours. Then, as the fog gradually cleared, things started to fall into place in her befuddled brain. He'd been so cold lately, almost like he was slowly freezing her out. It became crystal clear what that scene on the Bangkok flight was all about.

She reached for a box of tissues and blew her nose. Sitting forward again, she placed her shaking fingers on the computer mouse and moved the cursor to the search window. She typed in "Lettie" and watched as a long string of emails flooded the screen. They went as far back as the month after Susan and Mitch had arrived in Dubai. In one email, Mitch said he had sent the money she needed for her family. Susan's breath caught in her throat. Her hand shook as she opened the desk drawer and pulled out Mitch's bankbook. As she flipped through the pages, her eyes were drawn to an entry that showed a twenty-thousand-dirham transfer, but no indication of who it was sent to. She compared the dates of Mitch's email and the transfer. *What the hell? That's over five thousand dollars!*

A searing white anger took the place of the hurt as visions of the gifts he "thoughtfully" brought back for her from his layovers ran through her mind. Suddenly they took on a whole new meaning. They weren't sweet gestures but guilt gifts.

She picked up her phone to call him, then put it back on the desk. This wasn't something to confront him with over the phone. He wouldn't have boarded his flight yet, but she didn't want him to turn around and come back. His parents were counting on him.

She went back to each email and hit print. She pulled her shoulders back and exhaled loudly. She would have to wait until Mitch came back to have it out with him. If he deleted the emails in the interim, she would have hard-copy proof.

She was relieved to have a distraction for the meantime. She needed to get to the bottom of what was happening with Anu's friends and figure out Kan's full story. She had a gut feeling that what Kan had told her was only part of it. She would throw herself into uncovering the rest.

Her phone pinged. She looked down and saw a message from Pat.

— The police are here talking to Barry. Can you come?

~

The police were still there when Susan arrived at the hospital. She hoped it was because they were being thorough. The security guard at the door recognized Susan, opened the door, and ushered her in. The police turned and looked at her, then looked to Barry.

"It's alright, she's the friend my wife was telling you about," Barry began. "The one that was with her at the ski hill when the accident happened."

Pat interjected. "She was also with me when we discovered the break-in at the house." Pat smiled weakly at Susan. "And, she was here when that man tried to suffocate Barry." She reached for Susan and the women hugged.

"I may be able to remember some details that Pat can't." Susan directed her comment to the officer. "It's been a stressful time, to say the least."

The officer spoke directly to Barry. "Okay, she can stay," he said and pointed to a guest chair in the corner.

Susan bristled at being ignored and directed to sit again by an official. She felt dismissed. She was vibrating with nervous energy but knew most of it was because of what she had just discovered about Mitch. She should have gone for a run to work it off, but it was way too hot. She would make sure she got a half hour of rowing in later and maybe some lengths in the pool. She inhaled deeply and forced herself to sit quietly and listen. Doing otherwise would cause trouble rather than helping. It seemed like they were wrapping up anyway and didn't want her input.

"So, Dr. Thornton, we have a detail assigned to the hospital grounds and main entrance," one of the officers said. "We checked in with your CEO again today, and he plans to keep a guard posted at your door 24-7 until the perpetrator is found. The investigation of the break-in at your home is ongoing. We have not yet determined if there is a connection." He closed his notebook and put it in his breast pocket. "If we learn anything more, we will inform you." He nodded to his partner, and they left the room.

"Well, I'm not sure if I feel any better or not." Pat sat on the bed on her husband's good side. "Actually, I know I feel worse . . . and scared." She leaned over onto his chest, and he slowly wrapped an arm around her.

Susan could tell it was painful for him to do so. "Pat, be careful," she said. "I'm sure that's a bit uncomfortable for Barry." She stood and gently put her hand on Pat's shoulder as she sat up. "What did the police say?"

"They believe the chairlift malfunction wasn't an accident," Barry said. He shifted a bit. Pat sat up and he and reached for her hand. "There were traces of a detonation device in the twisted metal and debris." He shook his head. "The other person on the chair with me, Chris, an anesthesiologist here, died yesterday from his injuries."

Susan gasped. "How awful!"

Barry took in a shaking breath. "He died because of me. They weren't sure who the target was until the guy tried to finish the job."

A whimper escaped from Pat. "Barry, honey, who would want to kill you? You're such a kind and loving person, and an excellent surgeon."

He shook his head. "I have no idea who, but I think I'm starting to understand why. Not the full picture, but I just have to piece it together." His eyes started drooping. "I'm so tired."

"You need your rest," Susan said and rearranged his pillows. She gave him a half smile. "Sorry, can't help it. It's the nurse in me."

Barry gave her a weak smile in return. "I feel better with the security guard here, but I'm not sure I'll be able to sleep." He shifted again. "I need to talk to Anu and see if she has a file that I asked her to get in my office at home." He turned to Pat. "I don't want you mixed up in this. And until they've caught the men who broke into our house, I think you should go and stay at Susan's. If that's okay?" He looked at Susan.

"Okay, now you're scaring me. What's going on?" Pat asked. "Of course, I'll do as you ask, but you need to tell me. Anu told us something about her friend Sara who's missing, but we don't know why. Do you? She told us she asked for your help to find her and Kan."

"I'll tell you what I know when I know you're safe. Deal?"

"It's okay for Pat to stay with me," Susan said. She put her arm around Pat's shoulder. "I'll make sure she's safe. And you'll be happy to know that I found Kan, and she's okay. Is there anything we can do to help you?"

"You need to find Anu and my phone."

"That was actually next on my list, to find out why Anu didn't arrive at her friend's place. Someone must know where she is. I'll swing by Jan's massage parlor and check in again with the other girls to see if they've heard from her."

The door opened and Frank walked in.

"I guess the police have gone? What a shitshow!" He walked up to Barry's bedside and checked the IV line and monitors. "Dr. Thornton, you need some rest, and you ladies need to leave and let him do that." He pulled out a syringe and injected something into the IV port.

"Be careful," Barry mumbled as he fell asleep.

"What did you give him?" Pat asked.

"Just a sedative to help him sleep." Frank popped the used needle into the red sharps container. "Why was he telling you to be careful?" He turned to Pat with his hands on his hips.

"Oh, nothing really," Susan interjected. "Pat wants to prune some rosebushes, and Barry knows she always forgets her gardening gloves and the thorns . . ." She trailed off.

"Hmm, well, do be careful then." He looked at Pat and then back at Susan. "I'll walk you out." He placed his hand on Susan's shoulder and started to guide her to the door.

"No need." Susan gave her shoulder a tiny shake, and Frank's hand dropped to his side. "We know the way." She turned to Pat and reached for her. "Let's go get a bite to eat."

"I am a bit hungry," Pat said. "Frank, make sure Barry's never left unguarded."

"Of course." Frank motioned them to the door and stayed in the room as Susan and Pat left.

The door clicked behind them and the security guard straightened in his chair and crossed his arms. Susan gave him a brief nod and linked her arm through Pat's to steady her as she wobbled. *She's probably overdoing it*, Susan thought to herself but didn't voice her concern. As they passed the nurses' station, they both turned to the duty nurse, who abruptly spun her chair to face her computer and started typing.

"I don't like her," Pat whispered to Susan while they

waited for the elevator. "There's just something about her I don't trust."

"I get a bad vibe from her too." Susan sighed. "But she's probably just stressed. I remember those days. It's a tough job."

The elevator door opened and the women stepped into the empty space.

"Yeah, I guess. Earlier today I saw her and Frank talking with some official who looked pretty important," said Pat.

"Oh? A policeman?" Susan pushed the ground floor button.

"No, he was wearing a dishdasha and had some type of robe on top of that. He was carrying a folder with what looked like an eagle on it."

"Sounds like a federal ministry logo," Susan said. "I guess it's not unusual for an official to check in; hospitals are regulated by government agencies. Also not surprising considering one of their surgeons has been injured and an anesthesiologist killed in what is now looking like a deliberate attack."

"I suppose so," Pat said. "Then Becker showed up too. When he came along, Frank left. He didn't look happy."

"Well, with Chris's death the hospital administration is no doubt in a bit of a spin. Such a sin. I wonder if he had any family here."

The elevator doors opened and Susan stepped out, almost bumping into the woman set to enter the elevator.

"Nala?"

"Susan? . . . and Pat!" Nala reached for Pat's hand. "So good to see you. How are you doing? How is your husband?"

"Nala, hi." Pat took the hand that was offered. "It's touch and go, thanks for asking." The three women moved away from the elevator doors to allow others to enter. "I'm so sorry about the auction items. I—"

"Oh, please." Nala tut-tutted, still holding Pat's hand. "Don't give it another thought. We've already found other items that will bring in just as much. You need to focus on yourself and your doctor husband."

"Well, thanks, that's very gracious of you," Pat said.

"What brings you here?" Susan asked.

"I'm just here to talk to the hospital CEO about the gala," she replied. "There are programs, health clinics they're doing at the labor camps, that I think some of our fundraising could support."

"What a great idea," Pat said as the elevator door opened again.

"I'm glad to hear that," Susan said. "Well, let's not keep you from your meeting." She knew as well as Pat did that any fundraising had to be blessed by the government and the funds filtered through their chosen charity. It wouldn't do to alienate their benefactor. Nala was a great champion for those less fortunate. Then again, had she really been Kan's champion? From what Kan had told her, Susan had serious doubts.

"It was nice seeing you both." Nala swept into the elevator and turned, her gaze landing on Susan. "How was your trip to Bangkok? I mean, did you ever get there?"

"Yes, I did."

"Did you visit with Kan?" Nala put her hand against the door to keep it from closing.

"Yes, but very briefly. She's doing well." Susan wasn't about to offer any more details.

"I'm so glad to hear that. Come for tea soon and tell me all about it." She gave them a wave as she released the elevator door.

CHAPTER
TWELVE

The canvas canopy covering the back patio gave much needed shade from the scorching late afternoon sun. It was almost too hot to be outside, but the pool had a chiller, and a dip every fifteen minutes or so helped Susan and Pat keep their body temperature regulated.

Susan couldn't believe it had already been a week since Mitch had left. He had accomplished his mission and texted that he was looking forward to coming back. He was due home that evening. She could feel the anxiety building in the pit of her stomach at the thought of confronting him about the emails. Also, she had convinced a pilot friend of his to check his file in the mail room at work. Her passport had been there and he had retrieved it for her. She knew Mitch would be pissed but didn't care. It was hers, not his, and she may need it. She pushed the thought of the imminent battle aside for the moment and watched Pat climb carefully out of the pool, still protecting her injured ankle.

Pat had settled into Susan and Mitch's spare room and seemed to be doing okay, considering the circumstances.

The two women continued to spend several hours a day at the hospital, Pat more so than Susan, of course, but Susan remained hesitant to leave her for any length of time. There was still no word from Anu. Jan hadn't heard from her, and Hana and Mira didn't have any insight into where she may be either; May was not responding to texts. Susan had also been putting Nala off but knew she couldn't wait much longer to respond to her several invitations to join her for tea. She would have to go easy. Maybe Nala's husband was involved in what was happening with the missing girls. Maybe it was him Pat had seen at the hospital. Nala may or may not know. But why was she being so persistent? As far as Susan knew, Nala could be conspiring with her husband.

Pat sat on the end of her chaise and faced Susan. "Have you noticed that Miss Nasty Nurse hasn't been at her post the last several days? What's her name? I've watched her and Frank go at it. Seems they don't see eye to eye on some things."

"Her name is Carolyn, and I did notice she hasn't been there. Yeah, I've witnessed those heated discussions. I found it a bit unprofessional on her part, but I see how dismissive Frank can be with the staff. He doesn't seem the type to put up with insubordination. Maybe she got fired."

"Well, good riddance to her then. She was awful to both you and me, almost trying to keep us out of Barry's room half the time. I would think that having family and friends present would help in any patient's healing."

"It absolutely does," Susan said. She wondered if there was somehow a connection between the absence of the duty nurse and what was going on with Barry. She'd ask around and see if anyone could enlighten her on Carolyn's whereabouts. Maybe she was just on vacation.

Pat shifted to the middle of the chaise and swung her

legs around. "That swim felt good. I'd love to lounge here all afternoon and evening, but I should probably head back to the hospital. I'm so glad they're thinking of letting Barry go home in a few days. As it happens, our place is very accessible—no stairs to the entrance and all on one level, which is great for the wheelchair."

"Hmm . . . I still think it's too soon, but I'm not his doctor. And there's the question of security."

"The police will most likely organize a detail on the Palm, if they haven't already. And we can always hire extra private security." Pat stood and threw her towel over her shoulder. "Are you coming with me? You don't have to. I can drive myself, and you've already done so much."

"If you're sure, I don't think I will," Susan said. "I want to discuss a few things with Mitch when he gets home."

"Okay, I will get them to bring a cot back into Barry's room and stay there tonight, and likely until he's released," Pat said. "You and Mitch need some alone time, right?"

Susan hadn't told Pat about Mitch's infidelity. Her friend had enough to worry about, and Susan didn't want to dampen her enthusiasm about Barry's pending release from the hospital.

"Yeah, sure." She closed her eyes and sighed. She dreaded what was coming.

Susan was chopping spinach, bok choy, and ginger and tossing the mixture into the blender with a splash of almond milk when she heard the front door open and close.

"Susan, I'm home," Mitch called out.

She squeezed a long stream of honey on top of the mixture and turned the blender on high, not ready to engage. She steeled herself for the unavoidable confrontation. She had argued with herself the rest of the afternoon, sitting by the pool after Pat had left. Should she bring up his cheating or shouldn't she? Could she ignore it and go about her daily routine and put it out of her mind? She concluded there was not a chance in hell she could do that. At the best of times, she was a conflict-avoidant people pleaser who needed to be needed, but she had to face the music, as dissonant as it would be. She was sure their marriage wouldn't survive this, but she would see how he reacted. She glanced at the stack of emails she had positioned face down on the café table in the corner. She knew he would get a beer out of the fridge and sit in their cozy breakfast nook ready to catch up.

"Hey, hon." Mitch put his arm around her shoulder and kissed the top of her head.

"Oh, hey." Susan turned off the blender and wiped her hands on a towel. "I didn't hear you come in."

As expected, her husband reached into the fridge and grabbed a beer. "Are you ready for a glass of wine, or have you already had one?"

"No, I was waiting for you."

Her stomach had been acting up all day as it always did when she was stressed. She reached for the already opened bottle of cab sav on the counter. Her hand shook as she poured. She went to take a sip, but bile rose in her throat. She put the glass down and inhaled deeply and willed her stomach to calm down. She exhaled slowly.

"We need to talk."

"I know." He pulled out a chair and sat. "There's so much I need to tell you about my trip. Mom and Dad say hi, and so does Stan. They really missed seeing you."

"No, that can wait." She left her wine on the counter, walked over to the table, and sat across from him.

"Alright then, you first. What's up?" He took a swig of beer.

"First, I was at the airport and ran into Sergio. I asked him to check your mail file to see if my passport was there."

"Why? I could have brought it home. I checked my mail file and thought it was strange it wasn't there."

"I thought I might need it sooner."

"What for? What couldn't possibly wait until I got back?" He sat back. "And what were you doing at the airport anyway?"

She braced herself and kept her cool. "As I mentioned, one of the missing maids is from Sri Lanka. I promised Anu and her friend Mira I would help find her. So, I thought I'd take a trip to Colombo and was checking the flights. I got my passport but then decided against going. I didn't really have enough information to actually find her. I'm sure I could figure it out, but then, once I had my passport, I couldn't remember how to book a standby ticket. I asked Brad to help but then I couldn't remember the password to access the booking site and . . ." She was rambling, trying to defuse the anger she knew would be boiling up in Mitch, to match hers.

He exploded. "For Christ's sake, Susan! It's a damn good thing you didn't. Your passport is probably still flagged. Do you want me to lose my job?"

She bit her lip, trying not to lose her nerve. "Maybe that wouldn't be the worst thing that could happen."

"What the hell does that mean?"

"Well, we could move back home and get our life and marriage back on track. I think there are too many temptations for you in your job."

"Don't be so friggin' ridiculous." He slammed his beer down on the table. "Where do you get such crazy ideas? Your imagination is running away from you, just like it is with this lunacy with the maids. Just give it a rest!"

"It's not my imagination, in either case," Susan said quietly and pushed the papers toward him.

"What's this?" Mitch asked.

"You tell me."

Mitch turned the papers over and began reading. Susan watched the color drain from his face. She stood up, went to the counter, poured herself a glass of the green juice, then turned and leaned on the counter. Her heart thudded like it was trying to make a break for it, fighting against her stationary body rooted to the ground. If she didn't know better, she'd have thought she was having a heart attack.

Tears filled her eyes and started spilling down her cheeks. "Why?" she managed to squeak out.

Mitch slowly looked up and put the papers back on the table. "I don't—"

"Did she go with you to New Jersey?"

"No, of course not," Mitch answered with a hint of disbelief.

"Well? Can you blame me for thinking that? You both work for the airline, so it would be really easy to get her on the flight."

"I'm so sorry, Susan. You're right. There are so many temptations . . ."

"Do you love her?" She was focusing in on Lettie, not wanting to admit that she had found emails to other women, and photos.

"No, I don't, I love you." He walked over to her and reached his arms out. "We can work this out."

Susan wiped the tears from her cheeks, crossed her

arms, and stared up at him. "I'm not so sure." She shook her head. "You're not the man I thought you were."

She turned away and started rinsing the blender in the sink. Her shoulders shook from the tension building inside. She ground her teeth and felt like she would explode. She could feel him still standing behind her. It was so obvious now that it was a typical controlling behavior of his. He was close enough she could feel his breath on her neck. It was all she could do not to swing the heavy glass pitcher at his head.

"I'm sorry you feel that way and even more sorry I've hurt you." He walked away and sat back in the nook. "But we care about each other, and we've been together for so long. I think we'll be fine."

"Fine?" Susan shrieked. "Fine? What about the others?"

"Others?"

"Oh, Mitch. I found more emails and photos . . . and videos." She choked on the word. "I know it's not just Lettie, and it's been going on for a long time." Her voice rose an octave as she gained momentum. There was nothing stopping her now. "I wanted to stop searching, but the more I found the more it drove me on. You're such a bastard! And, a coward, and . . . and an imposter." She slid to the floor and sobbed into her hands.

Her sobs finally quieted down and they both sat in silence. After a few minutes, Susan composed herself and looked up. "I just don't get it. I thought we were happy."

Mitch shrugged his shoulders, defeated. "There's a part of me you don't know."

"Obviously." She let out her breath in a huff.

He put his head in his hands, then looked up and ran his fingers through his hair. "You must realize, we were kind of a mismatch from the beginning."

Susan was stunned into silence. Was this the same man she had loved for fifteen years to the very depth of her being, whom she'd always believed to be her soulmate? How had he hidden his "Mr. Hyde" from her for so long? She felt sick to her stomach.

"I'm sorry, I didn't mean it like it sounded." Mitch reverted to his "charming" voice. "Come to bed." He got up from the nook and reached his arms out to her. "We can talk about this more in the morning."

"Come to bed?" Susan's jaw dropped and she glared at him. She closed her mouth and clenched and unclenched her teeth. "You've got to be kidding. I can't even look at you."

She pushed his outstretched hands away and stood up. Her shoulders slumped. She shook her head and slowly walked down the hall and into the spare bedroom. Thank God Pat wouldn't be back tonight. She quietly closed the door behind her then sat on the edge of the bed. Her shoulders tensed as her throat tightened, holding back another sob threatening to escape. Why couldn't she yell and scream? Why didn't she slam the door? So many years of being the calm one in any situation—at home with two younger brothers and then her two younger cousins, and at work—had ingrained in her the need to tamp down her anger, leaving her unable to retaliate. She believed that once you started yelling, you've lost control. She would retreat into herself rather than lash out. Her go-to release when things built up was always tears, followed by overwhelming sadness, rather than anger. She was working on it, and the situation with Mitch was a huge test for her.

After a few minutes, she heard a light tap on the door.

"Susan?" Mitch said quietly to the closed door. "Susan, please come out. We need to talk this out." He paused.

"Please? It's over, I promise. I won't see her, or anyone else, ever again . . ."

Susan held her breath, silently pleading for him to go away. It was slowly dawning on her that she had chosen a lifestyle rather than a life partner. The romanticization of marrying an airline pilot, traveling to exotic places, the awe of the very fact that he had chosen her over anyone else. She had fallen for it, and the more she thought about it the more she realized she had turned a blind eye to all the signs and red flags.

Finally, she heard Mitch sigh, then the click of their bedroom door across the hall as it closed. She released the air from her lungs, along with a long, low moan. As the extent of Mitch's betrayal sank in, she felt a tingle gradually move up her spine and slowly envelop, then freeze, her heart.

Susan awoke to the sun streaming through the window and dancing on her eyelids. She had fallen into an exhausted sleep, leaving the curtains open. She was still fully clothed and on top of the duvet. At least she wouldn't have to wash the sheets if Pat came back to stay. Maybe she would suggest they both stay at her place on the Palm. Then again, Barry would probably be released in a few days, and Pat seemed determined to stay in his room with him until then. Either way, no need to worry about it right now.

She rubbed her eyes and glanced at the clock: seven thirty. She hoped Mitch had already left for the gym. He usually went on his days off. She hadn't looked at his schedule so wasn't sure if he would be working later or not. She wasn't ready to face him. *Thank goodness there's an en suite*. She splashed some cold water on her face. When she looked up, she was startled by the puffy-faced, red-eyed reflection staring back at her. She reached for a facecloth and ran it under the cold-water tap. She carried it into the bedroom, stretched on the bed, and placed the cold cloth over her eyes. Once she showered and pulled herself together, she would head back to the hospital.

And Mitch could go to hell. As far as she was concerned, there was nothing left to talk about.

CHAPTER

THIRTEEN

It was unusually quiet on the surgical floor. There were plenty of rooms free for surgical patients, so Frank had decided not to move Barry. The less this "drama" spread through the hospital, the better, he'd said. Since Barry's room was at the far end of the hall and around a corner, no one could see the security guard outside his door from the main hall.

Susan paused at the nurses' station, and a young nurse she hadn't seen before looked up from the iPad chart she was scrolling through.

"Hi, I'm here to see Dr. Thornton, Barry," Susan said and put on her most disarming smile. "Is Nurse Carolyn in today? I haven't seen her lately. Is she on vacation?"

"I just started this week," the nurse said. "I don't think I've met a Carolyn. Sorry." She stood up. "I'm told Dr. Thornton can only have family visitors. Can I have your name, please?"

"Oh, it's Susan. I'm on his approved visitor list." Susan gave a little wave over her shoulder as she walked away from the desk and headed down the hall.

She heard familiar voices.

"What are you doing here? Working on the fundraiser?" Frank's voice was unmistakable. "What does this lab have to do with the event?" His questions were coming rapid-fire, the volume increasing with each one.

Susan stopped and peeked around the corner of the hallway on the left just before the turn to Barry's room. She saw Frank standing with Nala under a sign that said: *Research Lab*. She hadn't noticed the sign before and wondered what type of groundbreaking research was going on. She knew it had to be big, as the UAE didn't do anything halfway. Susan pressed her back to the wall and kept listening.

"You have no need to know anything about it," snapped Nala. *What is she talking about? The fundraiser?* Susan hadn't realized Frank was involved in the event, but as a hospital administrator, she guessed he should be in the loop. She knew Nala to be a bit of a control freak, but speaking to a hospital administrator like that seemed a bit much.

The two headstrong personalities continued their heated conversation, but Susan didn't want to be caught eavesdropping, so she scooted across to the short hall where Barry's room was, hoping Frank and Nala wouldn't notice her. She slowed to a walk and smiled at the security guard.

"How are you today?" Susan asked. "Arun, isn't it? I hope it's been quiet."

"Yes, thank you, ma'am."

He stood and opened the door for her.

Pat got up and put her finger to her lips, nodding toward Barry sleeping soundly. She and Susan tiptoed out of the room, and Pat held her hand on the door, guiding it to a quiet click.

"How is he doing?" Susan asked.

Pat sighed. "He had a bit of a setback. He's developed an infection at the site of his IV port. I can't fathom how that could happen since they check on it so many times a day."

"It's not unusual," Susan reassured her. "He's very susceptible to infection right now, but since they do check him so often, I'm sure they caught it before it spread."

"I hope you're right. He's been sleeping pretty much since I got back. Frank says he'll have to stay at least a few more days. I just want to bring him home and forget all about this."

"I'm sure you do." Susan gave her a hug. "Sleep is the best thing for him. Shall we grab a coffee while he's still asleep? You could probably use a bite to eat too."

"I suppose I should, but I don't want to leave him for too long, okay? You can catch me up on any updates. Have you talked to Nala? Is there any news of Anu? I should pop by the house and get a change of clothes. Can you come with me a bit later to do that? I don't want to go alone."

"Yes, of course."

Pat turned to the guard. "I won't be long."

He nodded.

As Susan retraced her steps to the elevator, her mind raced through the new developments, not sure how much she should tell Pat. Most of it was speculation, nothing concrete. She'd do her best to fill her in without pushing any of Pat's panic buttons.

CHAPTER
FOURTEEN

The hot breeze ruffled the damp curls on the back of Susan's neck as the abra cruised the calm waters of Dubai Creek. Susan's childhood friend Chrissie chattered away beside her, filling her in on her research on the flora and fauna of the Arabian Desert. She droned on about how convenient it was to come visit, as the flight from Jordan, where part of her research was being conducted, to Dubai was much shorter than coming all the way from Toronto, where she was based, and how she was looking forward to the three-day conference where she was presenting a paper on the resilience of desert flowers, or something like that. Susan had zoned out when Chrissie, a botanist, had started to explain it. Susan had totally forgotten that she was coming in for a conference and that she had promised to give Chrissie a tour around Dubai the day before it started.

A ping on Susan's phone as she and Pat were having coffee at the hospital had reminded her that she was to meet Chrissie in Bastakiya to begin their late afternoon adventure. She invited Pat to join them, but she had under-standably declined. Susan felt guilty leaving her but a bit relieved that their coffee chat was cut short and that she didn't have to decide how much or how little to divulge of her suspicions.

It was never a good idea to explore Old Dubai in the heat of midday, so when visitors came, plans were always made for late afternoon or evening, or both. As frustrating as living in Dubai could be at times, Susan still loved to show off her adopted home and preferred to cobble a plan together herself rather than do the packaged tours. She had perfected an itinerary that began with wandering the heritage village in Bastakiya and taking in the Dubai Museum, then hopping on a local water taxi, an abra, typi-cally filled with Indian expats who worked in the many shops that dotted the banks on both sides of the creek, usually hidden from view behind the huge dhows unloading merchandise coming in from India and other foreign ports. After disembarking, she always took newbies to the Gold Souk. The bling-factor was off the charts, with wall-to-wall, floor-to-ceiling gold jewelry, one shop after another. The fish market was also a fun stop to make if she planned to cook at home. This time, the itinerary she had put together for Chrissie would culminate with an Arabian Desert adventure, complete with four-wheeling dune-bashing, followed by a barbecue under the stars, with belly dancing and henna painting, so no need to shop for dinner fixings.

It wasn't surprising that her usual enthusiasm was a little dulled by the circumstances of late, but she didn't want that to negatively affect Chrissie's enjoyment. She shook herself, tried not to worry about Pat and Barry, Anu and her friends, or her own doomed marriage, and turned her full attention to her animated friend. But the back of Susan's mind continued to whirr and sort through the events of the past several days. She couldn't shake the overwhelming feeling of foreboding creeping up her spine. She also wasn't looking forward to the gala tomorrow night. Pat had asked her to attend on behalf of the EWG. Susan totally understood why Pat wasn't up to going, but those kinds of events really put Susan on edge. She never felt like she fit in amongst the glitterati of Dubai. But, for Pat, she would do it. She'd have to dig her one multipurpose black cocktail dress out of the back of the closet for the occasion. It probably wasn't fancy enough, but it would have to do.

The abra clunked against the dock, and the people already standing swayed but, used to the motion, remained upright. Susan hopped off and turned to take Chrissie's hand to help steady her as she stepped on the gunnel of the small boat and straddled the two-foot distance to the wooden dock, then safely made the final step to land next to Susan.

The women laughed and linked arms and headed into the throng of shoppers mixed in with seafarers, weaving amongst crates and cloth sacks filled with everything from pashminas to dragon fruit and a plethora of spices. The pungent smells of cardamom and curry wafted around them, making Susan's mouth water.

"Hang onto me, I don't want to lose you." Susan tightened her elbow, bracing Chrissie's hand against her side. "It's just a few blocks this way." She pointed to the street perpendicular to where they stood.

"Lead on!" Chrissie's cheerful attitude was infectious, and Susan felt her tension disperse into the atmosphere around them, aromatic with heady perfumes one moment and odious with the body odor of sailors the next. It was an assault on the senses, but that added to the one-of-a-kind experience.

They started single file down the narrow sidewalk, allowing people coming from the opposite direction to pass. At the first corner, Chrissie stopped at a storefront to admire the window display.

"Shall we pop in here?" she asked.

"It's as good a place as any to start. Does something grab your attention?"

"That gold chain with the hand is pretty." Chrissie pointed to a piece of jewelry at the center of the display, hanging from an acacia tree also made of gold.

"That's an iconic symbol here," Susan said. "It's a Hamsa, or Hand of Fatima in Islam, or the Hand of Miriam in Judaism. You'll see it everywhere we go."

Susan's phone pinged. "Sorry, I'm just going to take a quick look. I have a good friend whose husband is in the hospital, and she's there by herself."

"No worries at all." Chrissie waved her hand. "I'll just get the shopkeeper to show me a few things." She walked over to one of the display cases.

Susan pulled her phone out of her purse and looked at the screen.

— Just wanted to make sure you're enjoying time with your friend and not worrying about me. I told Nala you would be going to the gala in my place. She was very gracious and understood totally. Thanks for doing that!!! I owe you! And Frank has offered to take me to the house to get changed and freshen up, pick up a few things for Barry, then back to the hospital, so I'm in good hands. See you tomorrow.

The hair follicles on Susan's scalp tingled. She wanted to type back that she would be right there to take her. Her fingers hovered over the screen. She stepped out onto the sidewalk and dialed the hospital instead and asked for the nurses' station on the surgical floor. After identifying herself, the duty nurse told Susan that Mrs. Thornton had left with Dr. Pettigrew, and they said they'd be back. Susan thanked the nurse and took a deep breath. At least there were people who had seen them. She was probably worried over nothing. She zipped her phone back into her purse and was about to enter the store when she saw a familiar face approaching. Carolyn the duty nurse was coming toward her, but her head was turned to the woman walking next to her. They were in deep conversation.

"Carolyn, hi!" Susan called. *What an opportune meeting.* The two women paused and turned to face her. "Anu? Oh my God, Anu! I'm so happy to see you. We've been looking everywhere for you." Susan reached out to hug her, almost forgetting the nurse in the excitement. She held Anu by the shoulders. "Are you okay? Where have you been?"

"Um, I'm fine. I've been staying with a friend in, um . . . Deira. I know Madame Pat isn't at the house, so I didn't think she'd miss me."

"I know it's been crazy, but Pat's been so worried about you. We all have. The last I saw you, you were getting on a bus to go to Jan's place. I went to see Jan, and she hadn't heard from you." Susan paused, remembering the nurse. "Carolyn, I gather you're no longer working at the hospital?"

"Yes, I've taken a position as an administrator, uh, at another hospital. A higher position and better salary." Her eyes darted across the street.

"It's funny running into you both here. I didn't realize you knew each other."

"Oh, uh, we, we don't really," Anu stuttered. "We recognized each other from that day at the hospital, when I hit my head."

"Yes, that's right," Carolyn added. "Well, it was nice to see you both. I'm afraid I have to run. I have an appointment . . . to be fitted for a new suit. I don't have many and in my new job I'll need some . . ." She did an about-face. "Bye," she said and waved over her shoulder and hurried back toward the creek.

Anu stepped back and waved to a young woman across the street. "There's May," she said. "It was nice to see you, Ma'am Susan. Please tell Madame Pat not to worry. I promise to go back soon."

"Okay, I will," Susan said and waved to the girl across the way. "Hi, May!"

May hesitated, then waved back as Anu ran across the street and grabbed her by the elbow, guiding her deeper into the market before Susan could cross to join them. *How strange.* Susan would have liked to talk to May and see how she was doing. She had been very quiet while Hana, Mira, and Anu had shared their stories. Susan wondered why May hadn't responded to her texts. Obviously she had been in touch with Anu. Susan couldn't really chase after them, and Chrissie was waiting for her in the shop. Susan would have to catch up with May another time.

In the gold shop, Chrissie had just completed her transaction, and the shopkeeper was fastening the Hamsa around her neck. Chrissie turned to Susan with a huge grin. She was obviously pleased with her purchase.

Susan smiled back while fighting down the acid reflux that marked the beginning of a burning sensation in her throat and chest. Stress often made it worse, and the chance encounter with Anu and Carolyn, and then seeing May, wasn't sitting right . . . or was it the souvlaki? She popped an antacid and linked arms with her friend, determined to enjoy the rest of their adventure. Next stop, the desert.

CHAPTER
FIFTEEN

The whirlwind tour of Dubai, from souk to desert adventure, was a resounding success. After dropping Chrissie off at her hotel, Susan had practically fallen onto her bed and into a deep sleep. Mitch was on a layover, so Susan was relieved to have returned to an empty house, a reprieve from facing that particular crisis.

She woke up early and after taking a soothing hot shower, put on a robe and headed to the kitchen. She took a large cup of coffee to the breakfast nook and admired the henna artwork done on the back of her hand at the desert encampment where she and Chrissie had feasted on chicken kebabs and watched a flurry of belly dancers and Tanoura dancers with illuminated whirling skirts. Her henna was an intricate piece of art that wove a riot of flowers and scrolls from the back of her hand up to her elbow. She knew anyone seeing it would suspect she had recently taken part in an Arabian Desert adventure or perhaps had been to an Arab wedding.

She had only been to one Arab wedding since she'd been living in the Middle East. It had been in Saudi Arabia when she and Celeste had gone there to find Tamara. Mitch had been right to be worried, but at the time, Susan couldn't think of anything else to do but accompany her friend and help to locate her daughter. Her deep-seated need to be helpful had overruled any concern for self-preservation, much to Mitch's chagrin. It had all turned out in the end, and Celeste and Tamara had happily returned to the States to get their lives back on track.

Susan often barreled headfirst into situations, without regard for her own physical or emotional safety, probably a carryover from her fierce maternal instincts to protect her brothers after their parents had died, and then helping out with her younger cousins too. She had felt an over-whelming guilt about the added burden they were for their aunt, compounded by the grief of losing both parents. She had thrown herself into looking after everyone so the extra bodies weren't too much for Aunt Margaret. Susan's dad was an only child, and her mother only had one sister. Aunt Margaret and her children were Susan and her brothers' last living relatives. Susan had lived in fear of being sent elsewhere if she and her brothers were too much. Now, years later and with no children of her own, Susan's need to nurture had to be directed elsewhere.

Susan gazed into the backyard. She loved the gnarly, creeping branches of pink bougainvillea that climbed up the back fence. One of the gardeners had cut them down to stumps a few months ago, misunderstanding Susan's request to "trim them back." She had been mortified to see the devastation and almost dissolved into tears, but she didn't want the gardener to feel bad, despite the fact he had made what she considered a grave error. Her neighbor, Joan, had called over the side fence and said not to worry, they would grow back even more beautiful, which to her great relief, they did.

Pat had sent several texts throughout the evening, catching Susan up on her visit to the police station. She and Frank had stopped there on the way back to the hospital. Pat said she'd save the details for when they saw each other. Susan was eager to get back to the hospital but decided to drop in on Nala first. She couldn't put off updating her on her visit with Kan any longer but resolved to tell Nala only the bare minimum.

She sent a quick text to Pat, ate a banana and some yogurt, and threw on some clothes, deciding to skip a workout. She paused and took several deep cleansing breaths, bracing herself for the day ahead.

"This is all I found," Anu said as she handed the manila folder to Nala.

Nala grabbed it and thumbed the tab that read *Research*. She flipped it open, pulled out two sheets of paper, perused them quickly, then shook them at her. "This is it? Where's the rest?"

Anu took a step back. She could see the telltale red blotches creeping up Madame's neck, a sign that the brewing anger could erupt at any moment. "There was no more."

"You'll have to go back to the hospital and ask Barry . . . Dr. Thornton." She thrust the thin file folder at Anu. "He obviously trusts you if he asked you to find this for him. You were smart to bring it to me." Nala paced the full length of the living room then back, stopping a few inches from Anu's face. She leaned in. "Show him this and ask if it's what he was looking for. Abdul says he was asking a lot of questions right before his accident, so he must have found something else. All that's in there," she jabbed her finger at the file, "are two barely legible pages—typical doctor chicken scratching. Just general notes about transplant surgery, from what I can tell." She huffed and resumed her pacing. "There must be more. I need to know what he knows before anything gets around. It's too soon to release my findings. I need more time to bring the board and the minister onside. This could ruin everything." She spun around to face Anu. "Not a word of this to anyone."

Anu took a few steps backwards, looking over her shoulder at the foyer, wishing she was anywhere but in this woman's house. It had started as a way to make some extra money. She didn't make much working as a maid and sent most of her salary to her family in Sri Lanka. When Anu had introduced Kan to Nala, Nala had asked Anu to help in finding other pregnant maids to be transported, and she'd agreed. After all, they had gotten themselves in trouble, hadn't they? Nala had convinced her they deserved to be deported back to their countries and would be better off in the long run. That's certainly what Kan wanted—to go home. Then, Nala's husband had asked Anu to do some work for him but not to tell his wife. He promised to help Anu get home and pay her a lot of money, in addition to what Nala was paying her, but she would have to work for them both in the meantime.

For every maid Anu told Nala about, she was paid two thousand dirhams, about five hundred US dollars, which was more than a month's salary. Then, Nala had approached her with another "business" proposal, a favor.

Anu gently rubbed the scar on her lower abdomen where they had removed her kidney. The stitches had only recently been taken out, and the incision was still red and tender. She fought down the sob that rose in her throat as she thought about her baby sister who had gone into kidney failure. There had been no help for her. She remembered how distraught her mother had been. Anu had told the story to Nala when she learned that Nala's son, Amir, one of the twins, was in kidney failure and on dialysis. Nala had asked Anu if she would help. Anu thought that no mother should watch a child die, so she agreed to be tested and was miraculously a match. Nala and Abdul had taken Anu and their son to a private hospital, where the surgery was done. It went smoothly and the surgeon had said since they were both young and healthy, recovery time should only be a few weeks. Anu had tucked away the ten thousand dirhams she had been paid and was going to use it to get herself home. She didn't trust Nala's husband.

"Where are you going?" Nala asked, stopping Anu's retreat. "You haven't had your tea."

"I told my friends I'd meet them . . . I – I really should be going."

"They can wait. We have business to discuss." Nala motioned for Anu to sit on the couch.

"Madame, I don't want to do this anymore," Anu began. "The other maids and nannies . . . they are talking and I—"

"The other maids aren't making the extra money you are," Nala snapped. "There's nothing to discuss. I need you to visit the hospital and tell the latest 'client' you brought in what she can expect. Reassure her it's all going to be fine."

"Please, Madame, I don't want to do it anymore." Anu started to cry. She regretted bringing May to Nala. She hoped May was doing alright.

"Oh, for heaven's sake," Nala said. She pulled open a drawer under the coffee table and took out an envelope.

"It's not up for discussion. I still need you. Here." She handed the thick packet to Anu. "That should help you keep going."

Anu looked in the envelope and her jaw fell open. She was about to comment when a bell chimed.

Nala called to her maid, "See who's at the front gate," then turned to Anu. "Hurry! Go upstairs and wait in the nursery with the children. They'll be so happy to see you. Read them a story or something." She shooed her through the foyer and toward the long staircase that led to the upper floor.

As Anu scurried up the stairs, she heard Isa say, "It's Ma'am Susan. She says you invited her for tea."

"Well, okay then. You can buzz the outer gate and let her in. Then show her to the library. We'll take tea there."

Anu paused at the top of the stairs before turning down the hallway to the nursery. She took a quick look through a small window above the door in the foyer and could see Susan coming through the front gate and into the garden.

"Go!" Nala hissed and pointed at Anu.

Anu disappeared down the hallway, opened the door to the nursery, stepped in, and quietly closed it behind her. Amir and his sister, Aila, ran to Anu and wrapped their arms around her legs. She hugged them back and wondered how long she'd have to hide.

Susan accepted the cup of mint tea Nala handed her and tried to quell the butterflies in her stomach.

"I'm happy to finally see you," Nala began. "I've been worried sick about Kan. Is she okay?" Nala busied herself smoothing invisible wrinkles from her kaftan then looked up and smiled at Susan. "And I'm so glad you'll be representing the expat ladies from the EWG at the gala tonight."

She sure can turn on the charm, thought Susan. She wondered what was hidden behind that forced smile. It was probably nothing. She was being paranoid. Here was a well-connected, highly respected Emirati woman who spent hours working on projects to raise money for charity and often opened her home for committee meetings and private dinners to encourage the wealthy of Dubai—and there were many, both expats and locals—to consider philanthropic contributions. Giving alms, zakat, was one of the Five Pillars of Islam, so Nala simply directed her fellow Emiratis to the charity she supported.

Susan had heard that Nala had gone to the UK for university, but she seemed content to raise her children and act the socialite. Susan wondered what she had studied.

"Would you like a biscuit?"

"Oh, yes, thank you." Susan reached for the plate and chose a chocolate-covered wafer.

"So, when you saw Kan, how did she seem?" Nala asked.

Susan took a bite of the biscuit, thankful for the brief pause to collect her thoughts.

"Well, she seemed relieved to be back home. But . . ." Susan paused, not knowing how much to divulge.

"But what?"

Susan made a quick decision to keep the details to herself for the time being. "It seems she lost the baby. She didn't want to talk about it, but it was obvious she wasn't pregnant anymore."

"Oh no! Poor Kan." Nala shook her head and reached for her tea. "The sweet girl must be devastated." She took a sip. "You know, even though it was an unwanted pregnancy, she had said she wanted to keep the baby. How sad. Did she say anything else?" Nala sat back and looked Susan in the eye.

"Nothing more about the baby." Susan squirmed just a tiny bit under Nala's stare but remained calm and held her gaze steady. She was used to being grilled by family members of patients in her care. "But her family has welcomed her back with open arms and appreciates her working at the restaurant. It seems to be a very popular place in a busy area, so I'm sure she'll get back on track." Susan popped the last bite of her biscuit into her mouth and chewed slowly, contemplating her next move.

Nala sat silent, gazing out the large sliding glass door overlooking the garden and an elaborate pool with a fountain of an elephant spouting water on one end and a twisting waterslide on the other.

"Is everything ready for the gala tonight?" Susan asked, breaking the silence. "If you need me to come early to help with anything, please let me know. Pat feels terrible she hasn't been available. It will be my pleasure to go on her behalf."

"No need for you to get there early. Everything is under control," Nala said. "Tell Pat everything is going smoothly. She has enough to worry about. How is Dr. Thornton doing?"

"He's doing as well as can be expected, I suppose, considering his injuries," Susan said. "You should drop in on him next time you're at the hospital."

"I suppose I could." Nala smiled and lifted the teapot and gestured to refill Susan's cup.

Susan shook her head and put her hand over her cup. "I'm sure he'd appreciate a visit, but I guess you'd have to get on the approved visitor's list to get past the security guard stationed outside his door."

"A security guard? Why?"

"Yes, there's one there 24-7. I thought you may have heard that last time you were at the hospital."

Nala shook her head and took a sip of her tea. Susan noticed a slight shake of Nala's hand, or was it just her imagination?

"I guess it's just a precaution while the police investigate." Susan sat back and watched Nala's face for any signs of . . . what? Guilt? Discomfort? "They're not sure the malfunction of the chairlift was an accident."

"Oh dear! Well, Alhamdulillah, let's pray he's on the mend and can go home soon. And that they can rule out any foul play." Nala stood up, indicating to Susan it was time to go.

Susan stood too and felt pins and needles. She had been sitting with her legs crossed for too long. She knew better but had been frozen in place; the tension from trying not to fidget had resulted in limited blood flow to her foot.

"Thanks for the tea and biscuits," she said, gritting her teeth as a throbbing took over from the pins and needles.

"Thank you for dropping by and updating me on Kan." Nala put her hand to her heart. "And, Dr. Thornton."

"You're welcome," Susan said. "I'll keep you posted."

"Thank you. My maid will show you out. See you at the gala."

Susan was dismissed.

~

Anu watched from behind the sheers in the upstairs nursery as Ma'am Susan made her way across the courtyard to the outer gate and onto the walkway along the road. She turned to close the gate and glanced back at the house. Anu spun around and pressed her back against the wall next to the window. Had Susan seen her? If so, Anu hoped with the sheer curtains it would be difficult to make out any specific features. Then again, did it really matter? She could just be there helping Nala with the children.

Her thoughts were in a turmoil, torn between feeling she had done the right thing and the squeezing around her heart that suggested differently. How would she feel if someone ripped her unborn child from her? She shook herself. She would never let that happen. Her body was not to be seen by any man other than her husband, if and when she got married. If you were with child and not married, that was a sin. She pushed away the thought that the women she had found for Nala had probably been raped, including May. No matter. They had to atone for their sins, didn't they? The inner conflict raged on inside her like a swirling typhoon. She wanted to call out to Susan but stayed silent and continued to fight down the guilt that was threatening to consume her.

Anu prayed that Ma'am Susan would figure out what was going on and notify the police soon, and prayed even harder that Nala wouldn't learn of her betrayal. At least not until she was safely home in Sri Lanka.

CHAPTER
SIXTEEN

Susan tried to keep her foot from flooring the gas pedal. She was already going fifteen kilometers over the speed limit, but cars were still passing her on both sides. She knew that the rules were applied differently for locals. They were rarely ticketed for moving violations, but expats were pulled over or caught speeding on traffic cameras on a regular basis, so she kept the speedometer hovering just above the speed limit.

She found a parking spot and sprinted toward the main entrance to the hospital, slowing down as she entered, not wanting to alarm anyone. Her nerves jangled and she had broken out in a sweat. Her usual creepy feeling had swarmed up her neck and wrapped its tentacles around her scalp during her visit with Nala. Her intuition was on high alert. Something was up with Nala, for sure, but Susan just didn't know what it was or if it had anything to do with Barry and his accident. Everything could easily be explained away. As the honorary chair of the EWG fundraising committee, Nala had every right to be at the hospital. The community programs run by the hospital administration, including those at the labor camps, would benefit greatly from the money raised.

She smiled and nodded at Arun stationed outside the door of Barry's room and wondered if he had been home since she had seen him last. He looked awake enough so she assumed so. She'd bring him a coffee and muffin later. She pushed open the door and was happy to see Barry propped up in bed with only one leg in a sling, the other leg still encompassed in a cast but resting on a pillow. She looked around the room and didn't see Pat.

"You're looking good today, Barry," Susan said. She reached down and gave him a hug.

"Hi, Susan," said Barry, returning her hug.

"Where's Pat?" She noticed the cot pushed to the side of the room and knew she was still staying overnight.

"She's here but went down to the cafeteria for a soup and sandwich. Apparently, the special today is minestrone, her favorite." He gestured to the visitor's chair. "Have a seat. She just left, so we have some time to talk before she gets back."

"Do you have an update from the investigation?" Susan asked. "Pat texted me that she and Frank stopped at the police station yesterday, but I haven't spoken with her yet."

"They did get an update, but there's really nothing new. At least nothing that the police are willing to tell us." Barry sighed. "I need your help, Susan. At least until I can get out of here."

"Okay . . ." Susan leaned forward. "What's on your mind?"

"Well, it's about a file I asked Anu to find," he began.

"The file marked 'research'? What about it?"

"I need to find it. That and my phone. I had notes and some photos on it." He held his hand up as Susan started to reply. "Let me finish, okay? I'm going to tell you something that I don't want Pat to know because it will only worry her more."

Susan nodded.

Barry took a deep breath. "I told Pat it was research for my work." He paused. "But there's more. I had a patient waiting for a transplant who had a rare blood type, and we didn't know if we would find a liver in time. It miraculously showed up at the eleventh hour, but we didn't have any information on the donor, which is highly unusual and would never fly back in Canada. I was told to just do the surgery and not worry about it. It was kind of the same when I was in Syria and Iraq. I learned there, and now here, to just keep my head down and do the work I need to do. The important thing is to save the patient."

"Who might that be?" asked a male voice.

Susan swung around to see Frank standing in the doorway. She hadn't heard him come in and wondered how much of their conversation he had caught.

"Oh, just a fictitious case study," Barry answered, cool and calm. "I was just asking Susan to pick up some of my files at home. I want to keep my brain active, so I might as well be studying possible scenarios."

Susan didn't feel calm at all but willed herself to remain so and smiled at Frank.

"You shouldn't be worrying about work," Frank said as he scrolled through the iPad in his hands.

"As soon as I have these casts off, I want to be ready to get back to the OR. I know you're short-staffed now."

"It'll be a while before you're wielding a scalpel again, my friend, regardless of what Becker thinks." Frank set the tablet on Barry's tray and started checking the lines running into his arms. "Looks like the infection is clearing nicely. Just a little red around the port but not as bad as it was." He flicked the stopper of one of the bags hanging on the IV pole. "How's your pain level on a scale of one to ten? It's been a while since you've had any pain meds."

"It's about a seven, but I don't want any more. They knock me out and it takes forever to clear the brain fog."

"Most of the brain fog is from your head injury, Barry," Frank said. "And if you don't manage your pain, your body will be busy focusing on that rather than healing."

Barry visibly bristled. "Don't patronize me, Frank. I'm a doctor, remember?"

"Right now, you're a patient," Frank said, unruffled. "And you'll follow doctor's orders. That would be me." He patted Barry on the shoulder, and before anyone could stop him, he had pulled out a syringe from his pocket and injected the pain med into the line running into Barry's arm.

"Frank!" Susan stood up.

"Susan . . ." Barry's voice trailed away as he fell into a medicated sleep.

Frank held up his hand. "It's for his own good," he said. "You said you were a nurse. You know it is."

Susan gritted her teeth, fighting back a harsh retort. "I just wish you had waited until he told me where to find the documents he wants me to bring."

"That can wait until he's better and released," Frank soothed. "He can read anything he wants and find them himself once he's home." He put his hand on Susan's shoulder, and she flinched. He dropped his hand and gestured toward the door. "We need to let him rest."

It was the second time in one day she had been dismissed. She stormed out of the room and went to find

Pat. It was a few hours before she had to go home to get ready for the gala.

At this time of the day Susan was surprised that the hospital cafeteria wasn't busy. Pat was sitting in her usual corner by the window with her chin in her hands, head tilted up, gazing into space. Susan called, "Hi, Pat!" and waved. She took the seat across from her, reached for Pat's hand, and gave it a squeeze.

"Boy, have we got a lot to catch up on." Susan reached into her bag and pulled out an apple. Her stomach grumbled in anticipation. "How are you holding up?"

"Just barely, to be honest. I've been trying those meditations Sherry taught us, but I can't keep out all the awful thoughts about what's going on."

"I know how hard this is," Susan said. "I just popped in on Barry, and he seems to be doing so much better. He told me you were down here. He was filling me in when Dr. *Frank*-enstein came in and gave him more pain meds. He really is a patronizing jerk."

"Oh, Susan. I think he's really just worried about Barry," Pat said. "He was so sweet yesterday, taking me home and then to the police station even though it was supposed to be his day off."

"Yeah, well, I guess I haven't seen the sweet side. It was good of him to take you." She took another bite of her apple.

"Unfortunately, the police didn't have anything new to report on the investigation," Pat said. "All they know is what they already told us—that the part that holds the chairlift to the cable appeared to be tampered with. They also told us that forensics confirmed the type of device used to create the explosion. The officer mentioned a bunch of technical terms about remote detonation I didn't understand. I should have written them down. Frank might remember."

"That seems like progress. I don't think they knew the specifics before. That could give them more leads, knowing any details about the technology the attacker used."

"I guess so but they were pretty dismissive."

"I know how that feels," Susan said.

"Oh?"

"Well, Frank just ejected me from Barry's room, and this morning, when I visited Nala, she kinda did the same. It was a short visit, and she seemed eager to get rid of me after she had been badgering me to come for tea. I guess I'll see her tonight at the gala and we can talk some more."

"What did you talk about?"

"Mostly about Kan, and a bit about the gala. Nala says she has everything under control."

Pat laughed. "I have no doubt she does. Even as 'honorary chair' she's done more than any other committee member. We're lucky to have her."

"Mmm, aren't we?" Susan wrapped her apple core in a napkin. "Well, I know Barry is going to be sleeping soundly for at least a few hours, and Arun is on the job. Do you want to go sit at his bedside, or can I take you out for a nice lunch? Barry said you were coming down for the minestrone, but I don't see an empty bowl here." Susan continued before Pat could argue. "I promise we'll be back before he wakes up."

"Actually, I think that's a great idea. I decided it was just too hot for soup, and I do need a change of scenery. They have my number if anything changes." Pat gathered her cup and napkins. "Can we go somewhere on the water? But close by?"

"Of course. I know just the place."

Late afternoon, the sun was still strong and the temperature hovered around thirty-eight Celsius.

"Jesus, it's so stifling," Pat said as they left the restaurant. "No matter how long we're here, I can't get used to it."

"Me either. Thank heavens for air-conditioning," Susan said. "It would have been nice to sit outside, but we'd be soaked through and then you'd freeze to death in the hospital's AC. At least we were at the window and could see the sea."

"You don't mind taking me back, do you? Do you have time before the gala?"

Susan glanced at her watch. "I don't mind at all. I still have plenty of time. I might even get a quick row in. My exercise routine is off the rails with so much going on."

"I'm so sorry to be monopolizing your time," Pat said. "I just don't have anyone else, really. You know, there will be other EWG ladies there tonight, so maybe you don't have to go."

"Don't give it another thought. I'm happy to go. Besides, being busy helps me keep my mind off my crumbling marriage." She paused.

Pat stopped and touched Susan's arm. "What's going on in your marriage? I thought you and Mitch were so happy."

"It's a really long story," Susan replied. "One I can't go into right now. I'll tell you all about it another time."

"I hope it's not because of us," Pat said, searching Susan's eyes.

Susan looked away. "No, it has nothing to do with you and Barry." She choked up. "But, let's not talk about it, okay?"

"Sure. But you know I'm here for you if you ever want to talk." Pat turned back toward the car. "What's that?" She pointed to Susan's windshield as they approached her Jeep. "If it's a ticket, I'm paying it."

"It can't be a ticket," Susan said and pulled the slip of paper from under her windshield wiper. "This is free parking for the restaurant."

She unfolded the paper and read it. Her eyes narrowed as she read it again. "What the hell? 'Nosy people have unfortunate accidents'?" She showed Pat the note and scanned the parking lot. "Well for shit's sake. I guess I've stepped on someone's toes." She chuckled.

"Oh, Susan," Pat said. "It's not funny—it's scary. No more amateur sleuthing, okay? I don't want you getting hurt. Let's just leave it to the police." They climbed in the car and buckled their seat belts. "We can stop at the station on the way back and show them the note."

"Pat, you said yourself that they didn't seem to care." Susan backed out of the parking spot and headed for the exit. "I'm invested in figuring this out now. For Barry and for Anu and her friends. I'm certain that it's all connected somehow."

"Please, Susan . . ."

"It's okay. I promise I'll be careful. I'll admit, I am worried, but I'm more pissed off than scared. Whoever it is can't get away with this."

❧

Susan arrived at the gala in plenty of time. She knew these events always started late, so the crowd was still fairly light. She smiled at the pretty young woman, in full harem-girl regalia, taking tickets at the door. The gala theme was Arabian Nights. Susan thought it was a tired old theme, but it always seemed to be a draw and did lend itself to a glamorous decor. At the last minute, she had wrapped a swatch of silk adorned with jingling coins around her waist—a hip scarf she had purchased for a belly-dancing class—to accessorize her boring black dress and to cover the wrinkles she hadn't had time to iron out, prioritizing a bit of exercise instead.

As she entered the ballroom, she pulled on the hem of her dress, trying to keep it from riding up. She scanned the room, looking for Nala. She wanted to make an appearance, say hello to Nala so she would know she had been there, and leave as quickly as possible, without offending. It was a fine balance.

She grabbed a glass of champagne from a passing waiter and took a long sip. The event was in a hotel ballroom, so they were permitted to serve alcohol. At a venue that wasn't already licensed, it was almost impossible to get permission, so most expat-oriented events were held in hotel event rooms. It wasn't just any ballroom. It was at the Burj Al Arab, touted as the only seven-star hotel in the world, even though the hotel star rating system only went up to five. *Very like Dubai to create its own scale*, Susan thought to herself.

She spied Nala chatting with the hospital CEO. She approached them, happy to be getting her official business done early.

Nala turned to her. "Hello, Susan. As-salaam alaikum." She bowed her head ever so slightly. "Do you know Mr. Alex Becker? The hospital CEO?"

"Wa alaikum as-salaam." Susan acknowledged Nala's greeting then turned to Becker.

"It's nice to meet you," the CEO said before she could say they had recently met.

His hand engulfed Susan's as he shook it in a brisk one-two motion while looking not at her but past her. "I see your husband," he said, turning to Nala. "If you would excuse me, ladies, I have business to discuss with Mr. Abadi."

Nala smiled and nodded as Becker disappeared into the crowd.

"I was just going to say we had met briefly in Barry's hospital room," Susan began, "but I guess he doesn't recognize me."

"He was probably distracted," Nala suggested. "And I'm sure he meets so many people. He will be thanking my husband for the rather large cheque that will be coming to the hospital after the gala for their community programs." She took Susan's elbow. "Now, come see what's on the silent auction table, and we can watch the dancers before we sit for dinner."

So much for a speedy departure, thought Susan. She caught sight of Frank on the other side of the ballroom and wondered if he'd be seated with them. She sighed and grabbed another glass of champagne from a passing waiter. Dinner probably wouldn't start until well after ten. It was going to be a long night.

~

Anu looked up at the sign that said *Private Research Laboratory – Restricted Access, Authorized Personnel Only* and felt her stomach do a flip-flop. She scanned the hospital hallway before punching in the code Nala had given her and, after one last look up and down the hallway, entered the lab. She hurried past a grouping of cubicles, where technicians hunched over elevated tables covered with an assortment of flasks and test tubes, none paying any attention to her. She noticed each cubicle had a small, steel-grey industrial refrigerator with glass doors and filled with an assortment of jars, some as big as a breadbox and others as small as a bottle of nail polish. She never looked too closely because she didn't want to know what they held. In her mind, "restricted" meant "secret," and that made her uncomfortable. She was never good at keeping secrets, and Nala had made it very clear that no one was to know about the work that was happening in the lab. And now she had to keep a secret from Nala too. She didn't really understand the work going on here, and Nala had told her very little. But she knew enough to be scared. It had gotten way out of control. What started as simply telling Nala about Kan's pregnancy had escalated into so much more.

When she got to the wall that ran along the far side of the cubicles, she pushed on the second panel from the right. It gave way and swung open to reveal a soundproof hospital ward, completely concealed from the rest of the lab. She walked to the last bed in the row. The chart hanging from the foot of the bed said *Dilation and Curettage (D&C)*, which Anu knew would be a pregnancy termination, and *Marrow Donor* in red at the top of the first page. Anu had no idea what that meant.

"May," she whispered. She sat down on the metal folding chair at the bedside of their newest donor. "Are you okay?" Her job was to keep the new girls calm and to explain to them that they would be compensated for their "donations." And that they were lucky not to be in jail. This was the first time it was someone she knew so well. As far as she knew, Kan hadn't spent any time in the ward and had been sent directly back to Thailand.

May struggled and pulled at the restraints wrapped around her wrists and attached to the bed railings. Anu stared at the restraints and her stomach did a somersault. She sat and held May's hand and whispered reassurances as best she could and explained what was going to happen. May nodded as the tears streamed unabated down her face. Anu did her best to assure her that she would be fine and reminded her that she'd be given five thousand US dollars and a ticket home when the procedure was completed. That seemed to have a calming effect, as it did for most of the girls.

Carolyn entered the ward and approached May's bed. She nodded at Anu.

"Okay, I'll be getting you ready for your procedure now," Carolyn said.

Anu hugged May and said goodbye. She stepped back and Carolyn administered a sedative into the IV line. May closed her eyes and relaxed.

CHAPTER
SEVENTEEN

Nala rearranged her hijab and tucked in a few wayward strands of hair. She took one last look in her rearview mirror and reapplied some lipstick. She opened the car door, grabbed her briefcase, gathered the folds of her abaya with her free hand, and swung her legs around. She didn't want to have this meeting with Dr. Pettigrew. Her lab was none of his business, at least not yet. It was unfortunate he had happened along just as she was entering the code. She should have used the back entrance, but when she checked, she hadn't seen anyone around. She was sure he had gotten a glimpse inside the lab before she noticed him coming up from behind her. She had closed the door, hoping she had blocked most of his view, but she couldn't be sure what he had seen. She had always flown under the radar, mostly allowing her people to do the hands-on work, but she went to the lab several times a week, usually at night when it was quiet.

She was happy to have hired Carolyn away from the hospital. Abdul had recommended her. She wasn't sure how he knew her, but Nala needed a skilled nurse to be in the lab when she couldn't be. Carolyn seemed very competent and didn't seem to have any type of loyalty to Frank or the hospital. Nala had asked her if she thought her bosses would be upset if she left. Carolyn had practically laughed and called Frank a pompous ass. Nala felt the same way. It had surprised Frank that she would have access to a restricted area. Wasn't she "just" a socialite fundraiser? He hadn't said those exact words but something to that effect, and that had made her blood boil. She would have to set him straight before he got even more curious, but she needed to do it quietly, one-on-one. She could tell he was annoyed that as head of surgery he wasn't privy to what was going on in that lab. The hospital funded a lot of private research and also made lab space available for projects led by the UAE government, so he had no need to be in the know. But, he would make a better ally than an enemy. She was very persuasive and felt confident she could bring him around to her way of thinking. The work she was doing in the lab directly benefited him and his patients. He just didn't know it yet. She looked forward to enlightening him further.

She would play the seniority card if necessary. The hospital CEO didn't bother her, and even her husband, who had helped secure the research grant, left her well enough alone, putting in an appearance for support when necessary, like at the gala. After she had worn him down, he had finally given in and agreed to let her do her "little lab project" as long as it didn't impact his carefully orchestrated life. He even promised to find her funding, which he did, in a roundabout way. To placate him, she had offered to help "repatriate" the maids who had gotten in trouble. She knew it was distasteful to him to have anything to do with it, but as an official in the Ministry of Human Resources, it was under his purview. She had convinced him that sending the maids back home was in keeping with her commitment to "helping those less fortunate." She didn't think he had made the connection between that and her "little project," funded through the Ministry of Higher Education and Scientific Research. He was too busy being important and kissing up to whomever he needed to in order to maintain his prominent position, which was precarious at the best of times depending on the way the wind blew in the upper echelons of government. He could be reassigned at any moment.

It didn't really matter to her. She had what she needed, and momentum was building, with the right people bene-fiting at the right time. She drip-fed both the hospital board and her government liaison just the right amount of infor-mation to keep them happy but not so much that they would ask too many questions. She included just enough technical-speak that their eyes glazed over and they moved on to the next agenda item. They didn't even need her at the board meetings anymore. It was just a rubber stamp now when the renewal of funding came about, as long as she kept them updated.

She fumed inwardly as she marched toward the hospital entrance. She hadn't spent ten years in university studying biochemistry to be a stay-at-home mom. Initially, her father had supported her in going abroad to university, promising her that he'd also support her in her career goals, but she knew deep inside that he hoped she would "get it out of her system." When she returned home, ready to take on the health care world and do groundbreaking research, she found that he had changed his mind and had succumbed to his well-entrenched traditional beliefs.

Mohammed Al Qasimi announced very proudly, shortly after her return, that he had found her a husband, Abdul Abadi, who was from a very well-respected family and was a good match for her. She was livid but he had insisted and even tried to soothe her by pointing out that the man he had chosen for her held a prestigious position in a high level of the government. She could help by doing fundraising work for the type of research she was touting and leave the "professionals" to take care of the rest. She'd argued that she was an expert in her field and just needed a chance to prove it. But her father's mind was made up. There was no use fighting it. So, she had decided to bide her time and vowed to herself that she would eventually make use of her husband's position and her family name.

As was the Islamic tradition, she would always be Nala bint Mohammed Al Qasimi and had kept her name as the daughter of Mohammed. She was okay with that tradition as she'd always enjoyed the respect the Al Qasimi name brought with it down through the generations, and it would be her name whether she married or not. But she was determined to make her own mark as a medical researcher.

She gave three short raps on the door with a plaque that read *Dr. Frank Pettigrew, Head of Surgery*. She had come too far, and no expat doctor was going to undo all her hard work. She pushed the door open, not waiting to hear an invitation to come in.

"Hello, Mrs. Al Qasimi." Frank waved her in and indicated the chair in front of his desk. "I have a surgery scheduled shortly so don't have much time."

"Dr. Pettigrew," Nala began. "Why don't we sit over here where it's more comfortable." She pointed to a couch and chair in the far corner of his office. She would gain control of this meeting, control that he had attempted to take by having his desk as a barrier between them.

"Very well." Frank stood up and came around from behind his desk. "Would you like a coffee?" He pointed to a side table with a kettle and a few Styrofoam cups. "I'm afraid it's just instant."

Nala wrinkled her nose. "No, thank you," she said and made herself comfortable on the couch.

Frank sat down in the neighboring armchair. "So, what can I do for you? Is this about the fundraiser? I hope the surgical team was well-represented at the gala last night, to your satisfaction. It was a wonderful event."

"That's very kind, thank you. We appreciate the support, and I was very pleased to see you and your team there."

"I also saw Mr. Becker there. As CEO, it's really his thing. Is it the use of the funds raised that you wanted to discuss?" He leaned forward. "That's not really my area of responsibility."

Nala gritted her teeth and fought back the urge to slap him across his patronizing face. "No, there's something else I'd like to discuss." She sat back and folded her hands on her lap. "It's about the research lab," she paused for effect, "*my* research lab."

"*Your* lab?" Frank sat back in his chair. "When I saw you there the other day, you didn't offer any explanation as to why you had access to the lab. As I said to you then, I should be informed of what's going on in my own hospital. You said it was none of my business." He let out a frustrated sigh.

"Yes, I'm sorry about that unfortunate exchange." Nala smiled. "And, yes, *my* lab. And, it's *Doctor* Al Qasimi." She reached into the briefcase she had set down beside her on the couch and pulled out a lab coat. She stood up and put it on. "Would you like to see it?" She was tired of hiding and wanted people to know she was a capable researcher who would soon be in the headlines worldwide.

"Yes, I would." Frank ran his hands through his hair. "But, how did you . . . ? I thought it was a restricted Ministry of Health lab."

"It is." Nala picked up her briefcase and headed for the door. "I'll explain as we walk."

"Okay, but I don't have much time. I have to prep my patient for surgery."

"I know," Nala said and turned to face Frank, her hand on the doorknob. "We're getting your patient's kidney ready now."

"Um, I'm not sure what you mean by that. I just had a text that it's en route."

"It is. If you come with me, I'll show you."

"Here we are." Nala punched in the six-digit code to enter the restricted lab, pulled the door open, and motioned for Frank to enter. "Welcome to my cryogenic research lab."

"Your . . . *cryogenic* research?"

"Yes, I studied biochem at Cambridge and worked on some pretty groundbreaking research in organ preservation. I was hoping to continue with it, but my father had other ideas." Nala turned to Frank with her hands in her pockets. "But, I did too."

Frank started to speak. "What does this have to do with—"

"Excuse me, Dr. Al Qasimi, I'm sorry to interrupt, but here's the kidney ready for implant." A lab tech handed

Nala a cooler marked *viable organ* and smiled. "The warm-up went perfectly." The tech stayed where she was. "And there's something else I need to talk to you about when you have a minute."

"Thank you, Tanya. I'll come to your station once I'm finished with Dr. Pettigrew." Nala took the cooler from her lab tech and turned to hand it to Frank. "I believe you have a surgery to get to?"

"Can I get a history on the donor? How do you know it's a match? Where did it come from?"

"I believe you have the paperwork. You'll see it's all in order." Nala walked to the door and opened it, dismissing Frank. "You'd better get to the OR; they'll be waiting for you."

Frank opened his mouth to speak and closed it again. He walked out of the lab and Nala closed the door firmly behind him. *That should keep him happy, at least for the time being*, she thought to herself. She made her way up and down the rows of cubicles, each with a lab tech testing various stages of the freezing and thawing process with organs harvested from animals. She nodded to herself as she passed each one, their backs to her and so engrossed in their work they didn't even look up to see who was passing by. *As it should be*, Nala thought. The testing on the human organs was behind the side wall, away from prying eyes that might question the ethics of it all. She was saving lives. That was as ethical as it got.

She opened the hidden panel in the wall and walked to the right where her most trusted techs worked with the stem cell hosts and the more delicate "organ resuscitation," as she called it.

"Okay, Tanya, what is it you need to talk to me about?"

"Well, I wasn't sure, but I just took a full inventory." She paused.

"And what did you find?"

"Some of the bags of blood with the enriched stem cells are missing."

"What do you mean? How can that be?"

Nala walked over to the steel wall behind the techs, a series of doors with dials and wheels. Behind each door was what looked like a combination of a meat locker and a bank vault. The doors all had a digital display that showed the inside temperature. Nala checked to make sure the temperature at the first vault was holding at minus 196 degrees Celsius. She glanced down the row and noted each vault's temperature gauge. Each one housed organs or stem cells at different phases of the research process. They were testing different temperature levels to determine the ideal setting for the best restoration outcome and different lengths of cryogenic stasis.

"I double-checked it, and based on the inventory of the bags we did three days ago, there are twenty missing. I didn't notice it because the missing ones are spread between all six vaults."

"That's impossible," Nala snarled. "Who would do that?"

Tanya shrugged and held out a full polar suit, and Nala stepped into it.

"What's the organ count?"

"I haven't counted those yet." Tanya handed her a face mask.

"Okay, you can go back to your station. I'll be a while."

Nala punched in a code on the first vault and spun the wheel while she mentally went through a list of people who had the codes to get into the lab and the vaults. She had kept it to a bare minimum, and she couldn't imagine any one of them stealing from her.

She thought about her beloved sister who had died so young from leukemia. If only someone had been doing research like Nala's back then, maybe they would have had a cure or treatment for her at the time. Nala was doing this in her sister's memory, partly. She felt that stem cell research was overregulated. She had started her cryo research mostly on stem cells but then expanded it to include lengthening the time for organ preservation. A liver once disconnected from its human body has about eight to twelve hours of viability before it needs to be hooked up to a new blood supply; a kidney has about twenty-four hours. Many people died waiting for a live donor or for someone to die and for the family to approve the harvesting of organs. There was research being conducted on cryo-freezing organs to allow them to be kept indefinitely, to be thawed on demand. But it was slow and the studies being done were using animal organs. There were none on human organs until Nala began her study.

Her son was alive because of her work. It brought Anu to her. He would have eventually gotten a kidney, but his body was struggling to tolerate the dialysis, so Anu being a close enough match and willing to help just sped things up a bit. Nala would have to make sure Anu knew how much she was appreciated. Nala would lure her away from the Thorntons to work in the Abadi/Al Qasimi home full-time. Nala needed to keep a closer eye on her. She also wondered just how much Dr. Thornton knew. It wasn't at all clear from the flimsy folder Anu had brought her. She hoped she could bring him on board. Then a creeping suspicion started to dawn. Were the attempts on his life somehow related to her research? She would have to talk to Frank, now that she was confident he would be in support of her work ... but that could wait.

She turned her attention back to the task at hand and walked into the deep freeze. She would decide what to do after Tanya's count was verified and she confirmed whether or not any of the organs were missing. Then she would visit her organ donors and see which ones were ready to be released and which ones they would keep behind to restock the inventory. It might be time to determine who might be a good "host" for generating more protein-enriched stem cells. It had never been done before with a human subject, and Nala was ready to try it. She had to choose subjects carefully. She would check their histories and see which ones didn't have family waiting for them back home.

She would make sure that Anu's friend May was sent home as soon as her pregnancy was terminated. She could use another of their volunteer donors for bone marrow. That should keep Anu loyal. It was a shame about the other Sri Lankan girl. But, there were those who had complications that were unavoidable.

EIGHTEEN

Susan's mind was going a million miles an hour. The rhythm of her footfalls helped her sort through the jumbled barrage of random, chaotic thoughts. She loved running at dusk on the boardwalk along the beach in Umm Suqeim, the slightly older section of Dubai that was a short jog from her front door. She preferred this quieter neighborhood to the bustling, crowded Jumeirah Beach. It wasn't as old as Bastakiya, but it was a slower pace and quainter than areas just a little farther north around the Dubai Marina and the Palm where Pat and Barry lived.

As she ran she mulled over the timeline of her investigation. *Investigation? Huh?* That was the first time she had thought of it like that. Pat had asked her to stop playing amateur sleuth, but maybe, just maybe, it was something she was good at. Could it be a new career path? She was sure she wasn't going back to nursing, so detective work might be worth looking into. Susan Morris, Private Investigator . . . PI. She liked the sound of that, but a career change would have to go on the back burner. For now, she would put her natural curiosity (some would call it being nosy) and her knowledge of psychiatry and the inner workings of the human mind to work on unraveling the mystery at hand. Most importantly, she needed to find out who was trying to hurt Barry and whether or not it had anything to do with the missing maids. She was pretty sure it did. She wanted to talk to Anu again. Seeing her at the Gold Souk was such a coincidence, even more so that she was there with Carolyn . . . and May. Susan didn't buy that Anu and Carolyn had just run into each other. Nala was acting strange as well. And Frank's erratic behavior seemed to be more than just concern about his top surgeon. Susan had a hunch that it was all connected, and she was determined to find out what, how, and why.

She slowed her pace to a jog then a fast walk as she approached the gate to her compound and started her cooldown. She waved at the gate guard and continued on. As she stepped into her air-conditioned villa, she sighed and paused to do a final stretch in the cool air. A quick swim would help her cool down.

In the foyer she caught sight of a folded piece of paper partly tucked under the bowl on the credenza.

She unfolded the note.

Susan,

I've gone to stay at Mike's for the time being.

Just call or text if you need me.

Mitch

No *X*'s or *O*'s, no "Love Mitch," just "Mitch." *That speaks volumes,* Susan thought as tears filled her eyes. It was both devastating and a relief that he wasn't there. He must have come home from his flight while she was on her run, changed, and grabbed a bag to go to his friend's place. She wouldn't call. She knew it was over. What was the point in rehashing all the evidence she had found? Mitch might say it was ironic that she was considering a career change to private investigator, if she ever decided to tell him. It was her determination to find the truth that led her down the rabbit hole of his cheating, not necessarily her prowess as a would-be investigator. He hadn't covered his tracks very well. Maybe he'd wanted her to find out. She'd never know, unless he chose to share that with her. For now, she would focus on helping Pat and Barry, Anu, and the other young women.

She changed into her bathing suit and headed out the back door to the pool. She hoped no one else was there. She knew she would have to catch Joan and Wanda up at some point, but for now, she just wanted to swim a few mindless lengths to tire herself out enough to sleep. The run should have done the job, but the adrenaline was still pumping through her system.

The pool deck was deserted. She dropped her towel on a chair and dove in and swam the full length of the pool underwater. She surfaced and spun around for another length as she did her best to empty her mind.

She'd deal with the rest of the shit in the morning.

F rank heard a quick, one-two-three rap on his door and braced himself—he had heard that knock before.

"Come in," he called.

Nala swept in even before the words were out of his mouth. He had gotten used to her graceful meandering around the hospital lately but had honestly slotted her into the "ladies who lunch" category. Obviously, he'd have to rethink his original opinion on how her presence could impact his life.

"Good morning, Dr. Al Qasimi." Frank motioned toward what he understood to be her preferred seating in his office. He had to level the playing field and find out more about this research going on without his knowledge, right under his nose. So, he would play her game, for now.

"Hello, Dr. Pettigrew. And, please, when we're alone, call me Nala." She smiled and sat in the middle of the couch.

"Okay, Nala." Frank lowered himself onto the chair next

to the couch. He didn't tell her to call him Frank. Not until he had a better understanding of what she was after.

"I just wanted to check and see how our, um, your patient was doing. Did the surgery go smoothly? Is the kidney doing okay? I mean, is the patient okay?" She leaned in.

"It went very well," Frank began. "We have the patient on the appropriate immunosuppression therapy protocols, and it will be some time before we know for sure if it will take, but all signs point toward a full recovery and fully functioning kidney."

"How wonderful to hear that." Nala sat back and almost clapped her hands but placed them on her lap instead. "I hope to work closely with you on many more transplant cases, but I need your help in presenting this latest case to the board."

"I don't follow."

"Well, that kidney you used yesterday is the first fully viable organ that we have successfully brought out of cryogenic freezing after being in stasis for several months. It's a huge step forward in organ transplant research."

"Okay . . . I'm sure the board will be happy to hear it was a success. And I'm eager to learn more about the procedures being used. I'm not aware of any research that has been successful in such long-term preservation of human organs."

"There isn't any. That's what makes it so exciting." Nala reached into her briefcase and pulled out a file. "The issue is they, the board members, don't really know about the specific details of my research or that we were that far along. They don't know that there was a surgery at this hospital yesterday using one of the organs from my lab. It's actually not the first. Dr. Thornton has done a transplant with one of our organs as well. But that one hadn't been in stasis nearly as long."

"How did the board not know? And why wasn't I informed before now?"

Nala ignored his questions and handed him the file. "I would like you to review these findings so you have some insight into the trials we have conducted. I hope I can count on your support." She sat back and let Frank flip through the pages. "I was also hoping that Dr. Thornton, as one of your top transplant surgeons, could be a champion for us, since I understand his patient's surgery was also a success, but then he had his unfortunate accident."

Frank felt an icy chill crawl up his spine.

"Unfortunate? Yes, I'd say it was. There was a fatality, and Dr. Thornton was seriously injured."

"Well, I hope he's on the mend," Nala said, with no response whatsoever to Frank's comment about a fatality. "I know he's a tremendous asset to your team." She started gathering her things and got up to leave. "We'll talk about this more later. I have to rush off to a committee meeting. I'll be in touch."

And with that she was gone in a flurry of flowing black robe and flapping lab coat, leaving Frank to his unsettling thoughts and a barrage of questions.

"To hell with this." Frank grabbed his lab coat and took off after Nala. He would get his answers now. Her meeting could wait.

As Susan stepped off the elevator and started down the hallway toward Barry's room, she saw a woman in a lab coat and abaya walking ahead of her. As the woman turned left, Susan paused. *Was that Nala? In a lab coat? That's strange.* Then she saw Frank emerge from his office, looking like a man on a mission. *He must be going to Barry's room.* But Frank also took a left, in the direction Nala had gone. Curious, Susan followed and peeked around the corner. She saw Frank take Nala by the elbow and steer her to the door of the research lab.

Susan watched as Nala entered the code and swung the door open. Once Nala and Frank disappeared inside, Susan hurried ahead and planted a toe next to the doorframe, stopping the door from clicking shut. She held her breath then peeked through the inch-wide crack and watched Frank and Nala go into an office at the back of the room, past a grouping of cubicles that looked like the configuration of a newsroom. She opened the door a bit further and took one step into the lab where she could see several lab techs with heads bent over workstations, holding a variety of vials, flasks, and beakers. Each desk had something like a small beer fridge with glass doors containing what appeared to Susan like some type of organ. Every other desk had a biosafety hood to keep out contaminants and protect workers from toxic fumes. She could see one of the techs wrapping a fine metal coil around what looked like a small kidney and lowering it into a centrifuge.

The tech turned and looked up at her. "Excuse me, can I help you?"

"Oh, um, no thank you," Susan stuttered. "I, um, I'm new here and I was looking for X-ray. I must have gotten off at the wrong floor. So sorry to disturb you."

She turned and slipped out the door, made sure it clicked closed, then speed-walked down the hall and toward Barry's room. As she took the corner she almost tripped over the security guard outside his door.

He was new so didn't know Susan. He stood up to block her way, narrowed his eyes while looking her up and down, asked for and scrutinized her UAE identification card, and checked a list on his clipboard at least four times. She shifted her weight from one foot to the other and willed herself to stay calm, hoping that Frank and Nala hadn't seen or heard her and weren't following. *What is going on in that lab?* She held her tongue and waited patiently until the guard grunted at her and waved her toward the door.

Before she could enter, Anu came around the corner, out of breath. "Ma'am Susan." She stopped as the guard turned to her and put his hand up.

"I said already, you cannot go in."

"It's okay, she's a family friend," said Susan.

"She still cannot go in." He stood his ground.

"Okay, fine." Susan put her arm around Anu and guided her away from the surly guard. "What is it? Are you okay?"

"Yes, I'm okay. I try to see Dr. Barry, and the guard won't let me."

"I know. They're limiting his visitors since the attempt on his life. Why did you want to see him?"

"I have the file he wanted." Anu pulled it out of her bag and handed it to her. "I went back to the house and found it under his desk."

"That's great, Anu . . . but when did you do that? Does Pat know you were back at the house?"

"Um, just maybe a few days ago . . . Ma'am Pat was here . . . I . . . I thought I could go in. I have a key." Anu started to cry softly. "I . . . it's my home, right?"

Susan hugged her. "Of course it is, I'm sorry."

"Can you take it in to Dr. Barry for me?"

"Yes, of course," Susan said. "I'll bring it in now. He'll be happy you found it."

"Okay, I will go now."

"I'll text you later then. Where will you be?"

"With my friend . . . in Deira."

Anu turned and hurried away before Susan could ask her friend's name. Susan looked at the file in her hand, then returned to Barry's door and knocked softly.

"Come in," Pat said.

Susan walked in. "Hey, you two." She forced her voice to sound normal. She was excited and worried all at the same time. The lab, the file—she didn't know where to start. "How are you feeling today, Barry? You're looking good. Even have some color in your cheeks."

"Yeah, feeling alright," he said. "But anxious to get the hell out of here."

"I bet you are." Susan leaned down and hugged Pat then pulled up a second visitor chair beside her. "Any word on when that might be?"

"Nothing specific," Pat said and put her hand on her husband's shoulder. "We are going to organize some private security before we go home." She sighed. "The police said once Barry is home, they will have a detail from each twelve-hour shift take a drive down the Palm and by our house a couple of times, but they won't be putting someone there 24-7."

"They seem to be losing interest in us," Barry said.

"That doesn't make sense." Susan stood up and started pacing, still gripping the file. "Aren't they concerned that there's a killer on the loose? Someone died in that 'accident,' and someone, probably the same person who tampered with the chairlift, tried to suffocate you!"

"They say the investigation is ongoing and that we need to be patient," Pat said.

"Well, you might as well be home," Susan said. "You'd be better off recovering in the comfort of your own bed."

"I feel the same way," Barry said. "Every time I start to come out of the fog and am able to think clearly, they give me more pain meds. I had to get mad at Frank again earlier today. I convinced him that my pain levels were manageable, and he finally gave in and left without pumping me full of opioids."

Pat chuckled. "He wasn't very happy about it." She leaned over and kissed her husband on the cheek. "Sure is nice to have you conscious and able to have a conversation."

Susan sat back down. "Yes, that's great progress. I'm glad to hear you're not having as much pain."

"I'm clearheaded enough to see you're holding a file. What is it?" Barry shifted in his bed.

"This," Susan held the file high with a flourish, "is the file you asked Anu to find." She handed it to Barry. "She was just here and wanted to bring it in herself, but the guard stopped her. I told her I would make sure you got it."

"That's great!" He flipped it open and his face fell. "Where's the rest?"

"That's all she gave me. Should there be more?"

Barry took a deep breath. He reached for a glass of water on the small table next to his bed and took a long sip from the bent straw. He was about to speak when the door opened and Frank walked in. Out of the corner of her eye, Susan saw Barry slip the file under the covers.

"Well, look at this. The gang's all here." He looked at Susan and gave her a smile that did not appear genuine. He walked up to the foot of Barry's bed. "How's the pain level now, Dr. Thornton? Are these ladies tiring you out?" He pulled a tablet out of his pocket and started reading and scrolling.

"No, they're fine," Barry said. "I'm enjoying the company, now that I'm awake and feeling better." Frank started to speak and Barry stopped him. "I don't need any pain meds, and I'd really like to know when I can go home."

"Good to see you almost back to yourself," Frank said. "Your vitals have been good, and if you really think you're strong enough, we'll consider releasing you in a few days. You'll still have the casts on but should be able to get around okay in a wheelchair." He swiped up the screen of his tablet and slid it back into his pocket. "Try to get some rest, okay? I'll check in again later." He turned to Susan and Pat. "Ladies, nice to see you. Susan, good to see you at the gala as well. Thanks for supporting our community programs," he said, then left the room.

"That guy gives me the creeps," Susan said after the door had closed. "I can't tell if he was sincere or if he really does appreciate the fundraising the EWG does. He's definitely not comfortable in a tux. Every time I saw him he was pulling on either his cummerbund or bow tie, head on a swivel looking like he was ready to bolt for any exit." She chuckled. "We were at the same table for dinner, he was seated across from me. He was sandwiched between two of the EWG ladies who were practically swooning over the handsome doctor. He barely said two words. All he did was nod. It was quite amusing to see him so uncomfortable."

"Ah, he's not so bad," Barry said. "Maybe a bit arrogant, but it comes with the territory. He's very good at what he does."

"So are you, and you don't come across so . . ." Susan couldn't think of the right word.

"Pompous?" Pat offered.

"I was thinking of something a little more insulting, but that'll do." Susan came around Pat's chair and topped up Barry's glass from a pitcher on the small table. "So, if he's not so bad, why were you hiding that file from him?"

Barry pulled the file out from under the covers. "I guess it's time I told someone about my suspicions."

Susan's eyebrows lifted. "Suspicions?" she repeated. Barry sat up and she fluffed the pillow behind his back.

"There's something odd going on around here, and it has something to do with a research lab on this floor. I know it's government funded, the sign outside the door makes that obvious, but . . ." He paused.

"Go on," Susan urged, while weighing all the pros and cons about telling them what she saw.

"It seems strange to me that as one of the lead transplant surgeons at this hospital, I'm not privy to what's going on. And Frank, as head of the department, isn't either."

Susan huffed out a breath. "I wouldn't be too sure about that."

"He told me all he knew was that the lab had been in operation for a couple of years, but up until about six months ago it was in the basement. Apparently, they needed more room so they took over some space that wasn't being used on this floor. I had never even heard of it before they moved it up here. Then I started seeing people leaving with coolers labeled 'viable organs' when our own patients were waiting for transplants. I know there's a national database that tracks and prioritizes people on the transplant list, so I didn't bring it up to Frank. But it still didn't sit right with me, so I took a couple of photos and even stopped one of people with a cooler and asked where the organ was going. They said they were just a courier doing their job delivering it to the heliport. Then I checked the transplant wait-list, and there was no record of anyone receiving organs on those dates."

"Sounds kinda fishy. Anything else?" Susan asked.

"Well, I had an opportunity to talk to Becker about a month ago at one of those 'welcome the new surgeon' cocktail parties. I had met him briefly at my own welcome reception but had a slightly longer conversation at this one. He's a different sort, but we actually found something in common. We're both avid skiers, so I invited him to join me on one of my regular Wednesday mornings. I warned him it wasn't like the hills he had been heli-lifted into but was good for keeping the legs limbered up, and the cold is a nice respite from the heat. He was skeptical but did start to warm up to me at that point. He says, 'Speaking of cold' and starts telling me about some groundbreaking research in cryogenics he hoped would be beneficial to the hospital. I asked if it had anything to do with what was going on in the lab on the surgical floor, and did he know anything about a liver that showed up out of nowhere for one of my patients. I also mentioned the couriers I had seen leaving with coolers marked 'viable organs' and that I had noted the dates and times, if he wanted them. His demeanor totally changed and then some government ministry guy joined us and Becker clammed up. Looked like maybe he'd been telling me something he shouldn't."

"Then what?" Susan prompted.

"Well, I started asking around and then thought I would get a closer look. I tried to see if I could get in, but the door was locked and there's a keypad entry. There's not even a window to peek in. I knocked and no one came, and then I saw a nurse coming down the hall looking very curious about what I was up to, so I walked away."

"Sounds mysterious," Pat said.

"That's what I thought. So, I kept digging." He pulled out two sheets of paper from the file and shook his head. "These are just a few notes I made about transplant surgery and what's happening in cryogenic research. The file also contained printouts of the photos I took of the couriers and a list of the dates and times. They're not here." He sighed. "And there's another page of notes missing."

Susan leaned forward. "What was on that?"

"Well, around the same time I was doing my digging, Anu had asked if I could help find her friend Sara."

"Yes, the Sri Lankan girl who went missing," Susan said. "Go on."

"Anu thought I could check this hospital and others to see if she'd ever been a patient. In the file was a list of the hospitals I had called and information on Sara, like her full name, home address. I was making calls from my desk at home and just slipped the page in the folder."

The all-too-familiar tingle on Susan's scalp was back. The break-in was definitely connected with Barry's accident. The file was what the intruders were looking for—Susan felt sure. They took the pages they needed and left the file so the theft wouldn't be obvious right away. If the page with Sara's information was also missing from the file, could there be a connection between her disappearance and the mysterious lab?

"Why didn't you tell me all this?" asked Pat.

"Well, Anu had asked me not to tell anyone about Sara, and as for the lab, there really wasn't anything to tell. It's hospital business—well, government business really—and medical research is competitive and proprietary. It's not unusual to keep it under wraps until there's a breakthrough. But then I was almost killed . . . twice . . . and I couldn't help thinking there could be a connection."

"I'm pretty sure there is," Susan began. "Seems someone doesn't want us to be asking questions."

"Us?" Barry asked.

"Didn't Pat tell you about the note that was left on my car windshield?"

"No, she didn't." He looked at Pat.

"You've been sleeping most of the time I've been here since then," Pat said. "And Frank's been coming and going and then Susan arrived, and then Frank came back again, so I really haven't had a chance."

"It's okay, honey. So, what was on the note?"

Susan took it out of her purse and handed it to Barry. He let out a low whistle.

"Oh shit," he said. "You need to stop poking around. Wait until I get out of here, and then we can decide what to do from there."

Susan nodded and took the note back and put it in her purse. She decided not to share the Frank and Nala scenario and some of the other details, like running into Carolyn and Anu down by the creek—at least not right now. While Barry was talking, she had decided she was going to find a way to get back into that lab to have a better look around. She had an inkling what was going on, but she would keep things to herself for the time being. Barry needed to heal, and there was no need to involve Pat. First thing Susan had to do was find Anu.

"I thought of somewhere else my phone could be," Barry said. "I think I put it in the inside pocket of my ski suit. They brought me my bag of personal effects after the surgery," he pointed to a counter at the side of his room, "but it wasn't in there."

"They likely cut your suit off when preparing you for surgery, and it was so damaged they didn't think you'd want it," Susan said.

"Well, we need to find it. It has the photos of the couriers and my texts with Anu about Sara."

The tingling on Susan's scalp escalated to a thrumming. She could see the connecting bits coming together in her mind between the secret lab, the organ transplants, and the missing girls. There were still so many questions, but if it was all connected, as she suspected, and the criminals had Barry's phone and had been able to get into it, then Anu's life was in danger too.

CHAPTER
TWENTY

The wind was kicking up, and in the distance a greyish-brown cloud was building from the ground, swirling and advancing. It didn't happen very often, but Susan knew it was definitely a shamal and it would envelop the hospital parking lot and the whole building and surroundings within minutes. She needed to get home and gather her thoughts. Home was in the opposite direction, so she felt she could stay just in front of the windstorm if she got a move on. She would also be safe there as the houses in her compound were built from heavy, solid concrete blocks. It kept the homes cool in the sweltering desert climate and also protected against the often blistering winds of the shamals. She started the Jeep and sped out of the parking lot.

As she took the exit ramp onto the highway she checked her rearview and saw the storm had already engulfed the hospital. She hoped they didn't lose power, although they likely had backup generators. She floored the accelerator as she merged into the oncoming traffic, which wasn't an unusual move on this multilane death trap. You had to be an aggressive driver or risk getting mowed down. The fear of the following storm increased her adrenaline tenfold. Her speedometer read 130 kilometers per hour—over 80 mph. Other drivers were still whipping by her, most likely also trying to outrun the storm.

The outer bands of wind were already buffeting the Jeep, so she increased her speed. *Only two kilometers to the exit. You can make it.* She gripped the steering wheel with both hands to maintain control of the vehicle and her emotions. She slowed only slightly as she moved a lane to the right in preparation to take the exit that would lead home. The visibility was getting worse as she made the last turn into her compound. The gate was already up and the security guard waved her through. She hoped he would be okay. The small guard shack probably wasn't very sturdy.

She pulled into the carport, and when she opened the car door, the wind ripped it from her grasp and flung it open. It took all her might to wrestle the door closed as needles of sand attacked her skin. She finally muscled the Jeep's door shut and, shielding her eyes, leaned against the wind that was funneling between the houses. It fanned out as it careened into the carport, creating a vortex of swirling sand and debris around Susan and the Jeep. She fought her way to the entrance that led from the carport into the safety of her villa. It wasn't the same safe space it used to be, but it would have to do for now.

She pushed the door shut and leaned against it. With her legs shaking, she slid down to the floor, wrapped her arms around her vibrating limbs, and finally let go of the pent-up emotions she'd held back during the drive and for the last few weeks. Her body shook as she released her tenuous hold, letting rivers of tears course down her cheeks.

She grieved the loss of her marriage, knowing it was too broken to fix; she cried for Pat and Barry, for the mess they were in; and she wept for Kan and the other young women. Barry would be fine. He had money and position. The maids did not and needed someone to give them a voice.

She may get deported herself, or worse, but she didn't care. If her gut was right, she was dealing with something unimaginable, and it had to end. But she needed to put a few more pieces together before she could go to the authorities. The police? The ministry? The sheikh's office? She would figure out exactly which authorities once she could prove her hunch.

She wiped her eyes and took three deep breaths. That always helped. She picked herself up off the floor and marched into the bathroom to clean up. She could hear the wind still howling outside, but it seemed to be calming down a bit. These storms came up fast and furious but also passed through and dissipated just as quick, much like the cleansing cry she'd just had. By the time she was showered and had a bite to eat, it would be completely done and she could head out again.

As she toweled off from her shower she heard five staccato raps on her front door. She smiled. It was code and she knew either Joan or Wanda, or maybe both, would be standing on the other side waiting for her two-knock reply. She grabbed the sundress hanging on the back of the bathroom door, threw it over her head, and ran to the foyer. She gave her front door two knocks in reply before she flung it open.

"Hey, girl." Joan leaned in to kiss both of Susan's cheeks. "We thought we'd check in and see if you're okay. That was quite a storm!"

"And, we brought libations," Wanda added, pulling a bottle of red from behind her back.

Susan laughed. "It's a bit early for that, isn't it?" She stepped aside to let her friends in.

"It's five o'clock somewhere," Wanda said and headed to the kitchen.

"Well, okay, just half a glass. You know where the corkscrew is." Susan opened the china cabinet in the dining room and pulled out three wineglasses. "I have to meet someone in an hour, but it's close by."

"Okay, fair enough. So, what have you been up to?" Joan asked, making herself comfortable on the couch. "We haven't seen you around much. Just the Jeep coming and going at all hours."

"Oh, it's a long story, but I'll give you the *Reader's Digest* version." Susan handed the glasses out and then held hers up for Wanda to pour.

"We're listening," they said, almost in unison.

After finally shooing Wanda and Joan out with a promise to fill them in further later, Susan left with only a few minutes to spare. She parked just outside another expat compound not far from hers. She pulled her phone out of her purse and reread Mitch's message:

— Taking some time off . . . going to Bangkok for a few days to clear my head. Can't stand to see you hurting. I'm so sorry. Call me if you want to talk. Mitch

She clenched her jaw and deleted the message. The last thing she wanted to do was speak to him. He was probably "clearing his head" with Lettie—both the big one and the little one. She didn't want to think about it right now; it was too much to even fathom that almost fifteen years of her life, or a good chunk of it, was a huge lie. She sighed and put that thought away to unpack at a later date.

She scrolled down to her text exchange with Anu. The girl had agreed to meet with her at the same playground where they'd met with May, Hana, and Mira a few weeks back. It seemed like a lifetime ago, so much had happened. She knew she could walk through the schoolyard next to the compound and onto the playground, avoiding the guard at the gate. It was really a false sense of security in many of the compounds. Few had walls around their full circumference. The ones that did probably housed some of the higher-ups—corporate executives—although the execs were mostly in huge villas with sprawling grounds behind very tall walls, or in high-rise penthouses and suites in the very best five-star hotels. The division between haves and have-nots was almost as blatant as the caste system in India, but none of the haves liked to talk about it for fear it would tarnish their otherwise happy existence. Her own was being tarnished more and more every day.

As she approached the swings and teeter-totters in the sandpit, she saw Anu sitting on a bench. Another girl sat next to her, but when they caught sight of Susan, the other girl stood up and moved to another bench on the opposite side. Susan didn't recognize her. There were only two children in the whole playground, probably too young for school, so Susan guessed the other girl was another nanny who worked in the compound.

"Hello, Anu, how are you?" Susan sat on the bench and took Anu's hand.

"Hello, ma'am." Anu pulled her hand away. "I'm fine." Her eyes darted around the playground and then dropped to her hands folded on her lap. "Did you give the file to Dr. Barry? What did he say?"

"He said some pages were missing." Susan paused and watched Anu's reaction.

Anu's eyes darted around the playground and out to the road. "I promise, that's all I found."

"It's okay, I believe you," Susan soothed. She was fairly certain that the men who had broken in to the house had taken the missing pages, but she didn't want to alarm Anu.

"I can't stay long. Ma'am Nala will be home soon, and I have to be there."

"Are you working for Nala now?"

"Yes, ma'am."

"I'm surprised. What about the Thorntons?"

"Ma'am Pat is not home now, and I think she would be okay for me to work for Ma'am Nala. I need to make money …" Her voice rose then trailed off.

"Oh, I'm sure she would understand," Susan soothed. Then she decided to get right to the crux of the situation. "Are you doing more with Ma'am Nala than just housework and looking after her children?"

Anu squirmed. "I don't understand."

"Well, I'm pretty sure I've seen you coming out of the restricted lab at the hospital." She hadn't, actually, but was playing on a hunch. "And I've seen Nala going into the same lab, so I can only assume you're there doing something for her. Unless there's someone else you're working for in the lab? And, is Carolyn working for Nala now too? Is that why you were with her at the Gold Souk?" Susan stopped short of asking about the missing pages again; she noticed Anu was squirming. "Anu, Dr. Barry's phone is still missing. He said there were texts from you on it with information about Sara. You need to be careful. I have a gut feeling this is all connected in some way. What do you know about that lab? Do the missing maids have anything to do with it?"

"I – I . . . have to go." Anu started to stand and Susan put her hand on her knee.

That was all the confirmation Susan needed. Anu *had* been in the lab.

"It's okay, you're not in trouble," Susan began. "Nala doesn't know I saw you, and she doesn't have to know you're talking to me."

Susan had to tread lightly. She didn't have a clue what Nala had Anu doing. She also didn't know how committed Anu was to Nala or what Nala might be doing to maintain the young woman's loyalty.

"Is she making you do things you're uncomfortable with? If you tell me, I can help you."

"Oh no, Ma'am . . . I mean, Susan," Anu stuttered. "I look . . . only look after the children . . . and . . . but . . ." Anu's eyes filled with tears as she scanned the playground again.

"But what? You can tell me." Susan held her breath, hoping she was getting through.

"I can't . . ." Anu shook her head and started shaking and crying.

Susan put her arm around Anu's shoulder. "Okay, shh." The girl was distraught, obviously scared. "You don't have to. But I need to get into that lab. I was able to get in very briefly, but I need to get back in."

Anu turned to her with wide eyes. "You were inside? You know?" she whispered. Her shoulders fell and she let out a long sigh.

"Know what?" Susan asked. Anu seemed relieved that Susan had been in the lab.

Anu shook her head.

"You don't have to say anything, but can you give me the code to get into the lab?"

Anu was still for a moment, then nodded. "It's Ma'am Nala's twins' birthday." Anu leaned over to Susan and whispered into her ear, then she jumped up and ran through the playground and onto the school grounds.

Susan watched as Anu disappeared down the sidewalk. Poor girl was scared to death.

The door slammed behind her before she could put her hand out to stop it. She didn't want Ma'am Nala to know she was back. She needed to think before telling her what Dr. Barry had said about the file. Anu had hoped she could sneak up to the nursery before anyone discovered she was back.

"Anu? Is that you?" Nala's voice floated down to her from upstairs.

Anu's heart flew into her throat. She sprinted to the stairs and took them two at a time. "Yes, Ma'am, I'm here."

Anu wondered why Nala was in the nursery and not in her library. And where was the tutor? She was usually there until suppertime. Anu slowed when she got to the landing, catching her breath. She glanced at her watch. *It's after five!* She had lost track of time.

"Where have you been?" Nala was standing outside the children's playroom with her arms crossed. "I've had to watch the children since their tutor left. She wouldn't stay a minute past five o'clock. I'll have to find someone else who is a bit more flexible for when you're out *gadding* about. It's a good thing I was home. Remember, you *do* work for me now."

"I – I'm so sorry," Anu stuttered. "I went to the hospital to bring the file to Dr. Barry, just like you ask me." She thought quickly about how she would explain she had given the file to Susan, but she decided not to mention Susan at all. "I was not allowed to go into the room so asked a nurse to give it to him."

"Well, that's not acceptable." Nala crossed her arms. "We needed to know if there was anything missing." She huffed. "Honestly, sometimes I feel I have to do everything myself."

"I'm sorry, Ma'am."

"Well, if you couldn't even go in to see Dr. Thornton, you should have been home an hour ago. Where did you go after you left the hospital?"

Anu's heart did a flutter. She'd never been very good at lying. "Um, I – I had a headache and took a walk to clear my head. I didn't realize it was so late. It will never happen again."

She reached for the doorknob, and Nala stepped in front of her. "Make sure it doesn't." Her eyes narrowed at Anu who stood stock-still, then Nala stepped aside to allow her entry. "They're just finishing making thank-you cards from their birthday party. You can help them finish and then get them cleaned up for supper."

With that Nala spun away and headed for her bedroom suite at the other end of the hall, and Anu exhaled. Her head spun with all the secrets she was keeping. It was getting harder to sort out who knew what and who she could trust with what. She wanted it to be over.

CHAPTER
TWENTY-ONE

There were very few cars in the hospital parking lot when Susan pulled in at four in the morning. Some of the spots were taken by piles of sand that had been swept up after the shamal. There would probably be another shift of laborers in blue coveralls who would descend on the parking lot like an army to clear the piles away before daybreak. She hoped there wasn't a night shift in the lab. She doubted it, since it was a government entity, but she couldn't be sure.

She reached into the back seat and grabbed the old lab coat she had dug out from the back of her closet. She had kept it from the days she'd worked as a phlebotomist to put herself through nursing school. She stepped out of the Jeep and put on the lab coat and felt in the pocket for her stethoscope, a cherished graduation gift from her aunt. She ran her thumb around the silver bell and thought about telling Margaret she wasn't going back to nursing. She didn't feel ready to do that just yet.

For the time being, she had to focus on the mission at hand. She would attempt to get in and out without being

184

seen. She counted on the night shift workers being sleepy, and if anyone did notice her, she hoped she would just look like an intern or resident getting some extra hours in. As long as there wasn't a night shift in the lab, her plan should go smoothly.

She threw back her shoulders, walked in the main door, and saw there was no one at the concierge's desk. Susan smiled to herself and pressed the up button on the elevator. When the door opened on the surgical floor she took the stethoscope out of her pocket and slung it around her neck. With the elevator door opening and closing so much in the run of a day, the nurses rarely looked up from their work. Susan could see one nurse in the supply room at the back of the nurses' station. She was facing the other way, and no one was at the desk itself. Susan hurried past and turned down the empty hallway toward the lab.

She did some deep breathing to slow her heart rate as she approached the door. She took a quick look up and down the hallway then flipped up the cover on the keypad. She punched in the six-digit, day/month/year code that Anu had given her, then pressed the unlock icon. She heard the bolt sliding, then she turned the knob slowly and inched the door open.

There wasn't anyone working in the cubicles she could see from the door, so with one more glance up and down the hallway, she slid in and closed the door behind her with a quiet click. She held her breath as she heard the bolt slide back into place, then took a few steps into the lab, straining to see to the far end of the cubicles. They were all empty. As she slowly moved farther into the forbidden space, she noticed large canisters along the wall to the right, labeled LN_2, liquid nitrogen.

She was glad to have worn her soft-soled nursing shoes,

which made only the quietest of swishes when she walked. As she made her way up and down the rows of cubicles, she took a closer look at each small fridge on the desks and confirmed her suspicions. Each one had a jar with an organ inside. Every jar had a label that read either *kidney* or *liver*. They didn't look like human organs. Maybe pig? She thought that was normally what labs would use when conducting this type of research. A logo on the mini-fridge doors had the name *CryoFreeze*. She had never heard of the company but would look it up when she got home.

So far, this wasn't enough to prove any unlawful activity. She let a breath out slowly between her lips and made her way to the side of the lab. When Anu had whispered the code to her, she had also told her to push on the panel second from the right on the wall that ran along the right side of the room.

Susan's hand shook as she pushed on the panel. Nothing. She pushed again. Still nothing. Then she leaned back and counted panels again. She sidestepped to her right toward the second panel and tried again. The door was on a rubberized spring with magnets, and the pressure of her hand pushed it in a couple of inches, then it released silently toward her, exposing the hidden ward Anu had mentioned. She walked in and the panel swung back into place with a soft puff, barely a sound. Susan froze, trying to process what she was seeing.

To her left was a long row of beds, many occupied by sleeping patients hooked up to monitors. The overhead lights were turned off, but with the glow of lights from the monitors, Susan could see that all the patients were female. She tiptoed down the row and looked at charts hanging on the foot of the beds. Each one detailed the procedures the woman had had or was going to have—D&C, nephrectomy, hepatectomy, stem cell host—along with release dates. Each chart had a patient number but no names.

Susan could feel tears well up in her eyes. These poor women. She turned and looked around the rest of the room. There seemed to be an office back at the beginning of the row that she hadn't noticed when she entered the hidden ward. There was a glow of light coming from under the door, but Susan's eyes were drawn to the far wall, past a small grouping of cubicles, where there was a series of flashing lights and illuminating numbers from digital displays on floor-to-ceiling steel refrigerators. She couldn't quite make them out and had just started toward them when the office door opened. *Nala!* Susan crouched between the last two beds in the row and held her breath. She heard the office door close, then the panel open and close again. She let out the breath she'd been holding and stood up. She glanced down at the young woman in the last bed who was looking at her wide-eyed.

"Oh my God, May?" Susan knelt down beside her.

The girl nodded. "Ma'am Susan, please help," she whispered. She shook her arms, rattling the bed rail.

"Shh," Susan said, putting her finger to her lips. "It's going to be fine." She began to unbuckle the restraints but paused. She wouldn't be able to get all of the patients out herself. And without any authority, she'd be stopped by security, and she was sure they wouldn't give her a chance to explain, even if she could. She didn't know what shape the rest of the women were in without doing a closer assessment. She would have to go for help. In the meantime, it was best to leave things as they were.

"I'll be back, I promise," Susan reassured the girl, then

looked down the line of beds and saw several frightened faces framed by crisp white sheets and pillows. They were all staring at her.

"Don't worry," she said a little louder so they could all hear. "I'll get you out of here."

She had no idea if they all understood her, but there seemed to be a collective sigh throughout the room that gave her the strength she needed. She would start with Barry. He would be angry that she had continued to "poke around," but when she told him what she had found, he would understand and hopefully have some idea of who could help.

"You've got to be shitting me!" Barry shook his head. "Are you sure?"

Pat sat on the edge of her cot in the corner, rubbing the sleep from her eyes.

"That's awful." Pat yawned. "And seems a bit unbelievable."

"I wish I was shitting you," Susan said. She walked over, gave Pat a hug, and tossed her lab coat onto the cot. "I'm sorry for the rude awakening, but we have to do something."

"Who would do such a thing?" Pat slipped her feet into her sandals. "Surely the hospital doesn't know what's going on."

"Barry, what do you think?" Susan asked.

"Well, it's hard to say. When I checked around, nobody seemed to know anything about it. Even Frank." He sat up straighter. "You say Nala is involved?"

"For sure," Susan said. "I've seen her coming in and out of there a few times, and she was in there just now."

"What the hell?" Barry leaned forward.

"Don't worry, she didn't see me."

"We have to tell Frank," Barry said.

"I think he's in on it too," Susan said. "I saw him going in with Nala just a couple of days ago."

"I find that really hard to believe. Maybe he knows about the organ transplant research but surely not about the maids being held against their will, forced to have abortions and organs harvested . . . Jesus, saying it out loud makes it more horrific. It's like a horror movie." He shifted to get more comfortable. "Look, you have to be even more careful now. I barely knew anything." He shook his head again.

"I agree," said Susan. "Whoever 'they' are, they tried to kill you, twice! And they already gave me a warning."

"So, what do we do now? Go to the police?" Pat moved to her husband's side and took his hand.

"I think it's time we see how much Frank knows," Barry suggested. "I've worked with him for a while. I think I'll be able to tell if he's lying."

"Okay, but he probably won't be in for a couple of hours yet. We have to do something quick. Those poor girls have already been through enough. I just want to get them out of there." Susan started for the door. "I need some coffee. The cafeteria doesn't open until six, so I'll go get some of that swill from the machine down the hall."

"I have some fruit and granola bars in my bag," Pat offered. "We can have a picnic here and try to put a plan together."

Susan opened the door and gave a start. "Oh! Uh, hi, Frank. You're here early."

"I was just about to say the same thing." He brushed past her and entered the room. Susan followed behind. "I have an early surgery scheduled. One of our patients who's been waiting on dialysis for a few months finally has a compatible kidney available, so I don't want to waste any time." He patted Barry's cast. "How're you feeling? I thought I'd check on you before getting ready for today's surgery. I didn't expect you to be awake."

"Hi, Frank," Barry said. "We need to tell you something. Or maybe more to the point, ask you about something."

"Okay, but make it quick."

"You might want to sit." Barry pointed to the visitor's chair.

Frank glanced at the cot. "Whose lab coat?" he asked.

"It's a long story," Susan answered.

"This better not be a wild goose chase," Frank grumbled as he and Susan made their way down the hall toward the lab. "I'm due in the OR in half an hour." He glared at her. "You still haven't explained what I'm supposed to be concerned about and how you have the code to the lab."

"That's not important right now. I need to prove to you what I saw, and then you can notify the police. Coming from you, the head of transplant surgery, will give it more weight than coming from me, just an 'expat wife.'"

It was just after six, and Susan was hoping there still wouldn't be anyone in the lab. She braced herself, entered the code, and again heard the satisfying scrape of the bolt. Frank raised his eyebrows at her.

"Entrez-vous." Susan stepped aside to let him in.

"I've seen this before, and Nala has told me all about

her groundbreaking cryogenic research to preserve organs. It has already saved one of my patients, one of Barry's too, and one more today, and maybe more that I wasn't even aware of." Frank sighed. "I've seen all this. There's nothing illegal going on."

"Do you know where the organs are coming from?"

"What do you mean? I didn't have time to ask any questions. I was expected in the OR. I assume they're from donors," he snapped.

"Yes, you could say that," Susan said. "Follow me."

Susan headed for the side wall and pushed on the panel second from the right. She stepped aside to allow Frank to look in.

"What the hell?"

"So, you've never seen this part of Nala's lab?" Susan asked.

"Jesus, no." Frank walked slowly into the hidden ward. "Who are these people?"

"These are your donors, Frank."

He turned to look at her, and in that moment Susan knew he had no clue what had been happening behind panel number two.

He walked slowly along the row of beds, and Susan followed behind. She gave the girls in the beds what she hoped was a reassuring smile.

"Don't worry," she said. "The doctor is here to help too."

He looked at a chart hanging on the foot of one of the beds, then up at Susan.

"Sweet mother of God," he said. "These poor girls."

"You should see this." Susan took his elbow and led him to the other end of the ward to the row of refrigerated vaults.

They were peering through the small windows of the first two vaults, faces pressed up to the doors with their hands cupped around their eyes, when Susan felt the hair rise on the back of her neck. Before she could turn around she felt a sharp blow to her head, then all was blackness.

TWENTY-TWO

Nala paced the full length of the large reception area outside the hospital CEO's office. Alex Becker had attended a recent hospital board meeting where she had shared some of her research results that led to the use of viable organs for their hospital's transplant patients. Then, at the gala, she'd had a longer conversation with the CEO, and he had also spoken with Abdul. She had never needed his, or the board's, approval, and even though there were government officials on the board, they rarely attended the meetings. The others, including Becker, were expats from all over the world. She would, however, need their support when going public with the results and needed to ensure they were all behind her and the groundbreaking research she was conducting.

She had no choice but to ask for Becker's help in determining who might have had access to her lab. And she would need his promise of complete discretion.

When she conducted her thorough inventory count, she had discovered that not only were several bags of her precious stem cells missing, but organs as well. Whoever took them wouldn't understand that the organs would not be viable unless they were properly regenerated. The ones that were missing were the most recently cryo-frozen so may have a chance at viability, but it was a delicate process that she was perfecting under very stringent protocols. She felt sick to think that after such painstaking harvesting and care, the organs would be useless.

"Dr. Al Qasimi, Mr. Becker will see you now."

"Thank you." Nala brushed past the woman and opened the door without knocking.

"Ah, Dr. Al Qasimi, how nice to see you." Alex Becker was coming out of the private bathroom at the back of his office, drying his hands with a paper towel. Nala noticed the smile he gave her didn't reach his eyes.

He dropped the paper towel in the trash can next to his desk, put his hand to his chest, and smiled. Nala smiled back, appreciating his cultural understanding not to shake a woman's hand unless she extended hers first.

"Mr. Becker, as-salaam alaikum," Nala said and put her hand to her chest. He was in her country, and she would not cater to any of his European traditions. "Thank you for seeing me without an appointment."

"Wa, um, alaikum . . . as-salaam," Becker said back.

Nala tried not to cringe at his stumbling attempt at the Arabic reply in his thick German accent. She could tell by the color rising in his face that he knew he had butchered it.

"It was a pleasure to see you and your husband at the gala," Becker said. "The hospital is very grateful for the money you've raised for our community programs." He smiled.

"You're most welcome, Mr. Becker," Nala replied. "But I'd like to talk with you about hospital security."

Becker took a seat behind the desk as Nala settled into

the visitor chair across from him. "Security? What about it?" He leaned forward, elbows on the desk and hands clasped.

"Well, I really didn't want to bother you with issues relating to the lab," Nala began. "As you know, it is government-owned, and operated under my supervision."

"Yes, of course. But if you have concerns about security, I'm glad you came to me."

"I thought you should know that some items have gone missing from the lab, and I'm hoping you can help me find who is responsible."

"What items?" Becker asked, relaxing back in his chair.

"That's not important right now. The important thing is to find out who entered the lab without my permission."

"How many staff do you have working there?"

"It isn't one of my staff." Nala again dismissed his question. "I completely trust everyone who works for me."

"Of course." Becker nodded. "So, how can I assist?"

"I would like a list of all employees, a copy of the visitor sign-in sheet, and access to the security camera footage." Nala paused and looked him in the eye. "And I would appreciate your complete discretion on this issue. My research is at a very critical stage, and I don't want anything to interrupt or negatively impact it in any way. I'm close to making an announcement, but it's still too soon."

"No need to worry. This will stay between us, for now." Becker turned to his computer screen and began typing. "There are no cameras on the floors, only at the entrances and exits, and we don't require visitors to sign in." Nala started to speak but Becker cut her off. "I'm printing a list of employees for you and can set up a meeting with our head of security." He turned to her as the printer beside his desk began spitting out pages. "Is that acceptable?"

"It's a start," Nala said and stood up. "I will be in the lab, so please bring the list to me."

She left his office and swept through the reception, fuming at his insolence. She had connections and, with one phone call, could topple him from his high-level administrative perch. For the time being, she would leave well enough alone. As long as he was useful to her, he could remain CEO.

When Susan regained consciousness all was in darkness. Her chin was resting on her chest, and she felt a constant throbbing rhythm, with a staccato jab that ran from the base of her skull, around her head, and back and forth between her temples. She fought the pain and waves of nausea, realizing she likely had a concussion. She lifted her head and opened her eyes. All she could see was thick gauze —a blindfold. She gagged on a balled-up cloth in her mouth, and she could feel what was probably packing tape wrapped around her head, holding it in place. Her hands were tightly tied behind her back, and her legs were bound at the ankles and knees, immobilizing her. She tried to scream but gagged again on the rag closing off her throat.

How long had she been here? She took a deep inhalation through her nose to calm the rising panic. She caught the scent of some type of antiseptic. She sniffed again. Okay, that was definitely the smell of bleach or some other powerful cleaning fluid.

She heard a moan coming from the other side of the room. She moaned back, the only vocalization she could manage, then dropped onto her side and shuffled her way toward the sound. She bumped up against something soft —she was sure it was a person—and there was another moan. She tightened her abs and pulled herself up to a seated position. She couldn't help but think to herself, it paid to stay in shape. There was no movement and the moaning had stopped.

Susan scooted backwards, hoping to find a wall to lean her back on, and slammed into something metal that tipped over and clattered onto the floor, emptying its contents onto her. She imagined a bucket full of dirty water and a germ-filled mop that now lay on top of her.

That's just friggin' perfect, she thought, then passed out.

Nala decided to skip the lab and headed straight home. Becker could hold onto his list and meet with security himself. She would follow up with him when she got back and see if he had any leads. She had a feeling that Anu might know something, or may have given the code to someone. But why? After all she had done for the girl, she really couldn't imagine Anu betraying her. She had been on board from the beginning. *Greed does crazy things to people*, Nala thought as she entered the grand foyer of her villa.

"Anu! Are you here?" She unwound her shayla and took off her abaya. She tossed them on a chair and headed for the stairs. "Anu!" she called, raising her voice.

"Madame, hello." Isa came into the foyer and picked up Nala's discarded garments. "Miss Anu has taken the children out to the pool. Would you like me to tell her to come in?"

"No, thank you, Isa." Nala waved the maid away. "I just

need to sit a moment. I'll be in my rooms. When they come in, please ask Anu to come and see me." She started up the stairs then turned. "Oh, and can you bring me a tea and some dates? Thank you."

Nala had to think about how to approach Anu. She didn't want to spook the girl. But if it was her who was stealing, or she knew who was, Anu would be dealt with accordingly. Nala couldn't abide disloyalty.

The knots in her stomach got tighter and tighter as Anu watched the children play in the pool. She hadn't heard anything from Ma'am Susan, and she was starting to feel guilty about betraying Ma'am Nala. Would God forgive her for what she'd been doing? She kept telling herself it was the maids who had sinned, not her. She did want them to get to their homes safely and didn't want them to suffer, especially those she had considered friends, like May and Kan. And where was Sara? At least she knew now that Kan was safely back in Thailand. She felt another pang of guilt. Ma'am Nala had assured her the girls weren't in any pain, and Anu had been present, helping translate, when they had agreed to being donors—aside from the abortions that were performed with or without their consent. But that would keep them from going to jail, according to Ma'am Nala.

Anu heard the sliding doors to the patio open and felt sick to her stomach.

Isa walked across to where Anu was sitting, dangling her feet in the pool. "Madame is home and wants to speak with you," she whispered. "She doesn't look happy." Isa glanced over her shoulder and back to Anu. "I will bring her tea and you can get the children out of the pool and to the nursery, then go to Madame in her room, okay?"

"Okay. Thanks, Isa."

Anu called to the twins to get out of the pool and toweled off her legs. The knots in her stomach had turned into a swarm of bees buzzing around her intestines, with sharp stings as her irritable bowel flared up. She regretted telling Nala she would leave the Thorntons' employ once Dr. Barry was home, and sometimes she regretted giving Amir a kidney. As she wrapped him in a towel and handed one to Aila, he smiled up at her. Little droplets of water hung from his long eyelashes. Why was it always the boys who were blessed with long lashes? Her heart melted and she knew she had done the right thing to save his life, even though she was coerced into it. Thinking about the lives that were being saved is what kept Anu from leaving. That and the fact that Nala now had her passport and kept it locked up in a safe in her home office. She explained that she had taken it in order to check on Anu's visa to make sure she could transfer it to work for another family. She told Anu she would keep her passport safe for her and return it when it was needed. Anu missed her family and just wanted to go home.

Her bowel gave another spasm, and she rushed the children into the house, hoping to make it to the bathroom in time.

CHAPTER

TWENTY-THREE

"I think we should call the police," Pat said. "Susan hasn't responded to any of my texts, and no one else I've contacted, including Anu, has heard from her since she left yesterday with Frank. It's been over twenty-four hours."

"Maybe her husband wanted to spend some time with her," Barry said. "We've kind of been monopolizing her."

"But Frank hasn't checked in either. Didn't you think it was strange when one of the OR nurses came here to see if he was with us?"

"I guess so, but he's all over the place. He does have more than one patient, Pat. The nurse didn't come back, so they must have found him. Maybe the surgery didn't go well. But I agree, it is worrying. Even so, I'm not sure the police will do anything. We don't have any solid information for them."

"What we have is two attempts on your life, and now two people are missing. I think that's reason enough to call them. It's new information for the case."

"Pat, there's no way to link the two, and until we can, we don't really have anything to report."

Pat turned at the sound of footsteps approaching Barry's room. The door flew open and Susan and Frank stumbled in. A man wearing coveralls started to follow them in, but the security guard grabbed him by the elbow and pulled him out of the room. Frank pushed the door closed, shutting them both out.

"Good God, what happened to you two?" Pat rushed over to her friend as Susan lowered Frank onto the cot beside Barry's bed. His head was caked in blood, and there were bruises on his face and wrists. Susan's cheeks were red and bruised and her head was a mass of matted curls.

"Call the police," Frank croaked.

Susan helped him lie back on the cot. "We need to get you a CT scan. But I can at least clean this up and see how big that gash is. I'm sure it'll need stitches." She went into the bathroom, and Pat could hear water running.

"Where were you? What happened?" Barry asked Frank, as Susan emerged with a wet towel. "We've been worried sick. The way you look, I'm surprised no one stopped you in the hallways to take you straight to Emergency."

"Thankfully we didn't encounter anyone on our way here," Susan replied. "We wanted to talk to you two right away. We'll explain everything, but first we need to call the police. And I need to charge my phone. I can't believe they, whoever *they* were, didn't take it from me."

Pat took Susan's phone and, swapping it with her own, plugged it into her charger. She started fishing around in her purse. "I'll call the detective who was here. He said to call if there was anything new. I'd say this qualifies. Ah, here it is." She quickly dialed the number on the business card and asked to speak to Detective Malik.

The others waited in silence as she spoke with the detective.

Pat finished her call and said, "He's on his way. He said to sit tight and not go anywhere."

While Susan tended to Frank's wound, she told them what she could remember of what had happened.

Frank cut in. "I turned just as Susan was assaulted . . ." He closed his eyes and winced. "But he was too fast . . . struck me," he stuttered, bringing his hand to his forehead.

Barry and Pat listened, wide-eyed.

"Did you see who it was?" Barry asked.

"He . . . had . . . a balaclava covering . . . his face." Frank slumped against Susan's shoulder.

"Frank, don't try to talk," Susan soothed and turned to Barry and Pat. "A janitor finally found us in the closet and let us out. I think he heard me knock over a metal bucket."

"Oh my God, look at your wrists," Pat cried.

"Let's not worry about me," said Susan. "We need to think about May and the others and how to get them out of there."

Nala agonized over her next steps as she waited impatiently for her meeting with Becker and the head of security. Her research was at a very sensitive stage, and she knew a breakthrough was imminent. She had started with the altruistic idea of assisting the maids who had "gotten into trouble" by helping them get rid of the unwanted pregnancy and smoothing the way to get them out of the UAE and back to their home countries. Then she realized she could make use of the embryonic stem cells to continue the work she had been doing as a research assistant to increase organ and protein shelf life using cryogenic techniques. So, she put the plan in place to set up her lab. The therapeutic use of stem cell–enriched blood to treat everything from Parkinson's to cancer, diabetes, osteoporosis, and more was being researched, but it was going slowly. Nala had begun using human hosts to research mass production of therapeutic proteins and wanted to be recognized for the work she was doing, but she wasn't quite ready to release her results to the world.

Convincing the maids to also donate an organ and bone marrow came later and, in Nala's mind, was a logical next step. It hadn't been much of a leap to go from harvesting the fetal stem cells to convincing the maids, with an offer of monetary compensation, to become organ donors as well. The possibility of harvesting human organs and preserving them indefinitely meant no organ would ever go to waste. Only about ten percent of people who needed a transplant got one; the demand far outweighed the supply. Ensuring a longer lifespan for harvested organs and stem cells was an incredible development in transplant research. Running tests using human organs was groundbreaking.

Since her lab and research were a secret, she had been able to test the length of time an organ could be cryopreserved and run trials of the process to bring it back to viability. Frank had unknowingly proven that the first regenerated organ that had been brought back after six months in stasis in Nala's lab and been transplanted into a human patient was a success. She had counted on his commitment to save his patient to distract him from asking too many questions.

The security breach could undo all of her hard work. She had to present her findings to the right people at the right time.

~

"Your story seems a bit crazy," Detective Malik said as Frank and Susan led the way to the lab. "The Al Qasimi and Abadi families are very highly regarded here, and I know of Mrs. Al Qasimi's good work in the community and with charities."

"*Dr.* Al Qasimi," Susan corrected.

"I thought it was unbelievable too, and I didn't even know that Nala, Dr. Al Qasimi, was doing research in my own hospital until recently," said Frank, walking much slower than usual. "I attended one of her fundraising galas and was impressed with the work she was doing to raise money for the hospital foundation but had no idea she was using some of the funding for transplant research. When she 'miraculously' produced a kidney for one of my patients, I didn't have time to question it. My patient was already being prepped for surgery. One of Dr. Thornton's transplant patients had gotten a liver out of the blue, but I told him things work differently here and just to be happy for his patient, who wouldn't have lived much longer without a transplant."

As they approached the lab, Susan could see the door was ajar. "Well, looks like we won't need the code. After what happened yesterday, it would have been changed anyway."

The detective stepped in front of them and held his hand up. He put his back against the wall and motioned for them to wait. He drew his gun and used the nose of the pistol to push the door open. He glanced into the lab, then pushed the door wider.

He turned back to Frank and Susan. "It's empty. There's

nothing here. Are you sure this is the room where you were attacked?"

"What do you mean there's nothing here?" Susan pushed past him into the lab and froze.

The rows of cubicles were completely empty. There were no centrifuges, no fridges. She ran to the side of the lab and pushed on the panel second from the right. It didn't budge. She ran down the row of panels and tried each one.

"I swear there was a hidden hospital ward back here, behind this wall! And large floor-to-ceiling freezer vaults."

"I saw it too," Frank said and repeated Susan's attempts to open a panel, to no avail.

As a wave of nausea threatened to overwhelm her, Susan slid to the floor, her back against the paneled wall. "They must have moved everything. But where?"

Frank also lowered himself to the floor and leaned his head on the wall.

"You both need medical attention." The detective pulled out a notepad and scratched down a few notes. "I'll get a team here to gather evidence, and I will visit Mr. Becker in his office and see what he knows."

"But there's no evidence left!" Susan put her pounding head in her hands. "She's going to get away with this."

"There's always trace evidence," the detective assured her. "We're also gathering evidence in the janitor's closet where you were being held. And your and Dr. Pettigrew's testimonies will help." He took a deep breath before he continued. "There's probably enough to bring Dr. Al Qasimi in for questioning, but I will warn you, unless we find more evidence, it will be your word against hers. Try tracking down one of the maids you say were being held."

"It would be our testimony *and* Dr. Thornton's," Susan

said. She decided not to bring up Anu. She was already on the police radar, and Susan didn't want her to get in trouble. She felt Anu had likely been coerced into working with Nala. "We believe Barry's accident must have had something to do with this. He said he was surprised to hear there was a liver available, because his patient wasn't anywhere near the top of the international transplant list. A courier just handed him the cooler without a word and left. So Barry started asking around to find out where the organ had come from."

"When he came to me I told him not to look a gift horse in the mouth," Frank said. "I've been on this side of the world long enough that I've learned not to question authority. I just put my head down and do my job." He shook his head. "I think Barry, Dr. Thornton, kept asking questions and stirred up a hornet's nest."

"I think you're right, Frank." Susan turned to the detective. "You might also want to question a nurse that used to work here. Her name is Carolyn." Susan paused, realizing she couldn't keep Anu out of it. She was key. "I'm pretty sure I saw her with Anu at the hospital, and then I saw them together at the Gold Souk too. When I greeted them, Anu made some excuse and crossed the street. I saw her approach a friend, another maid named May, who I saw yesterday in the secret ward."

"You didn't mention that," Frank said.

"It's been a bit of a whirlwind, and I can't keep track of who I've told what." Susan laughed and winced as a sharp pain ran across the back of her head.

"We'll follow up on all of that," Detective Malik said. "First, let's get you to the ER."

A uniformed officer appeared in the doorway and said something in Arabic that Susan didn't understand. She really would have to improve her Arabic if she was going to continue living in the Middle East. But that was a big if. The room began to spin, both from her head trauma and from the memory of Mitch's infidelities.

"My officer will take you to the ER to have your injuries taken care of," the detective said.

"I know the way," Frank said.

"I realize that, but if your story is true, and you were attacked and tied up, then your life is likely still in danger. I would be more comfortable if my officer accompanied you both. And it looks like your head is still bleeding." He pointed to a smear of blood on the wall behind Frank.

"He's right, Frank, your wound is still bleeding," Susan said. The blood had seeped through the bandage she had applied earlier. "You obviously need stitches, and a CT scan." She clapped a hand over her mouth and inhaled deeply through her nostrils. Her head was swirling. "I feel like I'm going to barf." Her voice was muffled behind her hand.

The officer returned with a nurse and two wheelchairs. Susan successfully fought another wave of nausea and allowed him to help her up and then onto the wheelchair. The officer nodded to the nurse to lead with Frank in his wheelchair, and then he followed behind, pushing Susan in hers.

Susan felt her phone buzz and reached into her pocket. It was a text from Anu.

— *Maids at new location . . . being sent home soon.*

Susan texted back.

— *What new location? Police here at hospital and lab is gone. Can we meet? Do you know where Carolyn is?*

Susan hit send before thinking about whether or not to confront Anu about Carolyn's role, if there was one. She gnawed on her lip and watched as the reply bubbles came and went, and came and went. Then, nothing. She sent another text.

– Anu?

Still nothing.

She and Frank were wheeled into an exam room together and transferred to side-by-side gurneys. The officer positioned himself on guard at the door.

"I'll go get the ER resident to come and examine you," the nurse said and left.

A few minutes later there was a knock on the door and the officer let the doctor in. The resident raised his eyebrows at the officer then turned to the patients.

"So, what brings you here?"

Susan answered, "We were both attacked in a lab on the surgical floor . . . he has a large gash on his head that requires stitches, and I believe we both have concussions."

Frank huffed. "I can speak for myself. I'm Dr. Pettigrew. I'm a surgeon here."

"I recognized you as soon as I walked in," the resident said as he put on a pair of surgical gloves. "Your reputation precedes you." He extended his hand and Frank shook it. "I'm Dr. Pattison. It's good to meet you." The doctor reached for Frank's arm and checked his pulse, then listened to his heart. "You say you were attacked? Here in the hospital?" He glanced back at the officer. "I guess that explains *him*."

There was another knock on the door and the officer let in the nurse who had brought Frank to the ER. Susan watched her prepare a tray with instruments and sutures.

Dr. Pattison pulled out a small flashlight from his lab coat pocket and checked Frank's pupils.

"Your vitals are fine, but your pupils are a bit sluggish. We definitely need to get a CT scan done to make sure there's no intracranial hemorrhage." He turned to the nurse. "Please take care of stitching Dr. Pettigrew's wound, while I examine his friend."

Susan bit back the retort that she was *not* his friend and held out her arm for the doctor to take her pulse. She would have to reevaluate her suspicions where Frank was concerned, considering he was attacked as well. She would reserve judgment, for now. She fidgeted and pushed a wayward curl out of her eye. The sooner this exam was finished the sooner she could get back to Barry's room and update the Thorntons, unless the detective had already done that. Maybe she should head to the CEO's office first, then Barry's room. The detective might not welcome her meddling, but she didn't care. She was way too invested to back off now. She wondered if the police had already called Nala in for questioning.

She glared at the doctor as he finished taking her pulse and prepared to flash the light in her eyes. Normally she had tons of patience for fellow health care workers, but not today. She didn't have time for this. She had to get to Anu and find out where the maids were being held. If they could convince just one to corroborate Susan and Frank's story, then they could arrest Nala.

"You have one pupil bigger than the other. Is that normal for you?"

"Yes, it has always been like that."

"Okay, well, you do have a nasty bump there. I'd like to keep you overnight for observation."

Susan gave as sweet a smile as she could muster and nodded, having no intention of staying. She wondered how she was going to get past the officer. He didn't look like he'd be easy to distract. And the fact he didn't speak English was a barrier to her exit strategy as well—there would be no sweet-talking him. Mind you, that was never her forte anyway.

The officer opened the door to a ward clerk who wheeled in a portable X-ray machine. In the shuffling around of people and gurneys and equipment, Susan found her opportunity to sneak out unnoticed. Sometimes being petite had its advantages.

CHAPTER
TWENTY-FOUR

Nala flipped through the multiple pages of employee names and contact information that Becker had handed her. She looked up to see both him and the head of security watching her. Their smug looks proved they weren't really interested in helping her. She couldn't wait to have those looks wiped from their faces when she got them both fired.

"I'm not sure how helpful that list will be," Becker began. "I'm afraid there really is no way to determine who might have gone into *your* lab without authorization."

He paused and took a sip of his instant coffee. Nala crinkled her nose in disgust and was about to respond to his condescending comment when the intercom on his desk buzzed.

Becker picked up the handset. "Yes?" He paused to listen and his eyebrows knit. "Oh? Did you tell him I was in a meeting? Well, okay, send him in." He put down the phone. "It's a police detective. When my assistant told him I was in a meeting with you, he said he wanted to see both of us."

Before Becker could get to the door it opened and the detective strode in.

"As-salaam alaikum, Mr. Becker, Dr. Al Qasimi, I'm Detective Malik." He put his hand to his chest.

"Wa alaikum as-salaam, detective," Nala responded, hand to her heart.

He turned to Becker's security man. "And you are?"

"This is my head of security, Mr. Weber. He was just leaving," said Becker.

"Oh no, he should stay." The detective waved his hand. "He should hear this too, if he's responsible for hospital security."

"We should sit where it's more comfortable then," Becker said and motioned toward the salon area of his expansive office. "What is this about?"

Malik took his time wandering the office, looking at plaques and framed letters that adorned the walls, picking up and replacing soapstone carvings. He pushed aside two of the larger pieces and picked up a ceramic bowl with intricate patterns of random gold lines running around it. Nala's eyes widened as she thought she recognized the piece. The intricate art form was a very popular trend in Dubai at the moment, so it was certainly a different bowl, but it was very much like the one that was meant for the gala's silent auction, the one that was stolen from Pat Thornton's house. Becker didn't strike her as a very discerning art collector; he obviously preferred clunky, vulgar soapstone carvings. They were more reflective of his personality. She watched as Malik placed the kintsugi bowl back on the shelf. Her eyes followed him as he settled himself in one of the large wingback chairs.

Nala regained her composure and sat herself in the

chair opposite Malik, forcing Becker and Weber to sit on the couch.

"I am here because of a report of an incident that happened here yesterday."

"What kind of incident?" Becker asked.

"One of your surgeons, a Dr. Pettigrew, and a visitor, Susan Morris, were attacked, tied up, and locked in a janitor's closet."

"Excuse me?" Nala leaned forward. "Dr. Pettigrew and Susan Morris? When did this happen?"

"Are they okay?" Becker asked and leaned forward. "I heard Dr. Pettigrew didn't show up for a scheduled surgery yesterday and it had to be canceled. Where did you find them? Uh, where are they now?"

"They're being examined in the emergency room," the detective replied.

"Weber, go and check on them in the ER, and take a security guard with you," Becker ordered.

Weber stood up to leave, but the detective held up his hand.

"Not necessary, Mr. Becker. You," he nodded at Weber, "sit, please. I have one of my officers with them, they are safe. We must discuss the issue of a lab on the surgical floor. I am told there could be some potentially illegal activities. What do you know about that?" He looked straight at Nala, then Becker.

Nala sat up straighter and stared back at the detective. "My lab is on that floor, and I assure you there's nothing illegal going on. What does that have to do with the attack on Dr. Pettigrew and Susan? Besides, I don't believe you would have any jurisdiction over a lab sanctioned by the Ministry of Health."

"Technically not," Malik replied, "but the victims were

locked up in a closet on hospital property, which *is* my jurisdiction. As the police are a government department, we do often work with the various ministries when there are security issues. I think this would qualify, don't you agree?"

"Perhaps," Nala said. "But you still haven't explained why my lab would have anything to do with the attack."

"They claim they were in your lab when the assault occurred."

"That's not possible. They would need my authorization and code to enter the lab." Nala's heart started to race. Frank must have watched her enter the code when she'd brought him to see the lab.

"Well, I don't know about that, but we've just been in the lab." He paused. "The door was open, so entry was simple. And, it was empty."

~

Susan looked up and down the corridor to make sure there were no other cops wandering the hallways. She jogged to the entrance to the stairwell. Her head pounded and the thought of walking up four flights brought on another wave of nausea, but she didn't want to run into Detective Malik or his sidekick in the elevator. She hoped the officer was still watching over Frank and the detective was still with the CEO. She wanted to fill in Pat and Barry before the police caught up to her and locked her in a room again, "for her own protection."

Arun was seated outside Barry's room. She smiled at the familiar security guard as she approached.

"Madame?" He stood up with his clipboard in hand and blocked the door. He fumbled with the pages attached and ran his finger down the list.

"Hello, Arun, how are you today?"

"Um, fine, Madame." He stayed in front of the door, still blocking Susan's entry. His eyes darted from his clipboard to the floor, not making contact with Susan's. "You can't go in. You have to go." Arun stared at the wall ahead, shifting his weight from one foot to the other.

"What's wrong? You know me, it's Susan." Susan reached past him for the door.

He blocked her. "I'm sorry, Madame, family only."

"Don't be ridiculous, I'm here every day." She reached for the door again.

He sidestepped so his large frame blocked the entire door. "I don't have your name." He crossed his arms and stared straight ahead.

Susan's scalp started to tingle. "Okay, fine." She backed off. "I guess you're just doing your job. I don't understand why I'm not on the list anymore, but I will call Dr. Thornton's wife, and we'll get this sorted out." She hadn't seen this side of Arun before. She shivered.

She already had her phone in her hand and was dialing Pat's number. It went to voicemail. The tingling sensation spread up to the top of her head, circled the crown, and trickled back down her neck. Something didn't feel right. She shook it off. Pat had probably just turned off her phone to let Barry get some rest. Susan had to think very carefully about her next move. She could go straight to the top and tell the CEO to make sure she was added back to the list. That would be her excuse, anyway, to barge into the administrative offices. But what if Detective Malik was still there? Maybe that would be best. She had to have an ally somewhere in all this mess. He seemed her best bet. She knew that as an expat, she had to tread lightly.

As she contemplated her next move, she wandered to

the end of Barry's hallway and turned into the main corridor. She heard a loud voice coming from the hallway leading to the lab.

"Where the hell is my lab?"

Nala.

"Are you sure there was a lab here?"

Detective Malik.

Susan walked down the hall to the open door of the lab then stood listening just outside it with her back to the wall, debating whether to make herself known.

"Yes, there was a lab here," a third party with a German accent chimed in.

Ah, Alex Becker. That would make sense. At least he was confirming what she and Frank had already told the detective.

"Were you not informed, Dr. Al Qasimi?" Becker asked.

"Informed of *what?*" Nala spat.

"I was about to tell you when the detective interrupted our meeting. I contacted the ministry and requested the lab be moved to another facility, as we need the space. I was sure you were aware. I thought with the security breach, it would be best for everyone. I'm sorry if this is a shock."

"That's not possible . . . Who would have authorized that? They would have to run that by me! My research is at a very delicate stage. You've probably destroyed everything!"

"You should speak to your husband. He was the one who helped secure the grant funding on your behalf, wasn't he? I don't really remember. The board reviews so much paperwork . . . But I do believe he was one of the signatories, as it's a collaboration amongst several ministries, is it not?"

Susan didn't stick around to hear any more. She needed

to think. Most importantly, where were the maids? How did Anu know the lab had been moved and Nala didn't? She headed back to the ER to gather her thoughts and check on Frank, this time on the elevator. The more she thought about her exchange with Arun, the more her scalp tingled—although maybe it was just the blood sloshing around in the huge hematoma on the back of her head. No, there was something off about him for sure. Susan prayed she would be safe in the ER exam room for the time being. They were likely searching for her, and the officer on watch would be pissed. She would tell him she'd had to go to the bathroom.

She couldn't shake the feeling that Barry and Pat were in danger. For once, she wouldn't charge headlong into battle. When she got back to the ER, she would demand to see Detective Malik, and tell him to check on Barry. They couldn't stop him from going in.

CHAPTER

TWENTY-FIVE

Anu huddled in the corner of the playground, Ma'am Susan's words of warning ringing in her head. She texted May.

– I wish I was going to Sri Lanka with you now. Sorry for bringing you to Ma'am Nala. Please forgive me.

She waited and watched the bouncing reply bubbles.

– I forgive you. I have money now so can help my family.

The text was followed by a smiley emoji. Anu smiled to herself and wiped the tears that rolled down her face. She had been surprised to get a text from May. She hadn't recognized the number so she must have been given a new phone. Mr. Abdul had promised Anu that the maids would be okay, so maybe the new phone was from him. She had run some errands for him, but Mr. Abdul told Anu not to tell Ma'am Nala. She didn't want to do it anymore. He told her he would make sure she got home and gave her passport back to her. He told her to pack her bag and wait in the nursery. She asked if Ma'am Nala knew, and he told her not to worry.

218

She texted again:

- *How many maids are with you?*
- *Only 4*
- *Where are the others?*
- *I don't know*
- *Ok . . . have a good flight. I hope I see you at home soon.*
- *Ok bye*

She patted her pocket and felt her waist, making sure her passport was still there and the money belt was firmly in place. She was tired of being pushed around, one day threatened and the next day offered more money. At first, the money was enough to keep her quiet. Her family was so poor it was a big help to them. But she wanted it to end. The guilt was eating her up. She didn't know whom to trust. She would go to the police and hope they would help her. But first she would talk to Ma'am Susan. One thing she did know, she wasn't going back to Nala's.

Nala burst through the front door. "Anu! Where are you?"

Isa rushed into the foyer. "Hello, Madame. Anu is not home."

"Where is my husband?" Nala growled and tossed her abaya at Isa.

"He is in his study, Madame."

Nala flew across the living room and burst into her husband's study.

"How dare you?" She stood in front of his desk, her hands on her hips and chest heaving. "It's *my* lab. You have no right!"

"Oh, my darling, but I do," he replied and smiled. He

narrowed his eyes at her. "Why don't you have a seat and we can discuss this calmly." He motioned to the chair on the other side of the huge mahogany desk he sat behind. He leaned forward and clasped his hands. "You've been spending far too much time away from home and away from our children. I thought it was for the best."

Nala's anger deflated like a balloon popped with a pin. She dropped herself onto the chair. "But, why? I thought you supported my research. It's going to change lives."

"I do, and I'm very proud of you," he soothed. "But the hospital needed the space. And the ministry will be taking a more hands-on role moving forward and will consult you as needed."

"Consult me? It's mine! I need to see this through. How will they know what to do?"

"Your research assistants and lab technicians are all in place and will continue what they were doing. Your very detailed notes were all in your office, so that will help. It's all under control. As I said, they will consult you when needed."

"What about all the organs? If they weren't properly transported, they will be destroyed." She started to cry from frustration. She had to make him understand. She furiously wiped the tears from her cheeks. He wasn't going to break her. "Where are my donors?"

"Donors? More like prisoners." He sat back and crossed his arms.

She stood up and put her hands on his desk. "You were the one who helped with their transport, and we discussed how their 'unfortunate' situations could be turned around for the greater good. You also worked with immigration to facilitate their exit when they were ready to go." She paced the length of the room and back. "You even had Susan

Morris's passport flagged so she couldn't get back in the country when she returned from Bangkok. Or at least to stop her from asking so many questions. We know that didn't work. Probably because her husband works for the airline."

"Yes, that's all true."

Nala's eyes narrowed at her husband. "Did you have something to do with the attack on her and Dr. Pettigrew? Or Dr. Thornton's accident?"

"Of course not." Abdul sat back in his chair. "I have no idea about those unfortunate incidents."

"Well, we can discuss that more another time or leave it with the police. My lab is my main concern. I demand to see my donors. Where has my lab been moved?"

"I'm afraid that information is highly classified, but I'll do my best to get you clearance, my love."

Nala sank back into her chair, seething. She would bide her time. He would eventually have to bring her to the new lab. They needed her.

"Where is Anu?" she asked. "I need to speak with her."

"Anu? She's in the nursery. I left her there with strict instructions not to leave."

"Isa says she's not here."

The color drained from her husband's face. "You'd better find her," he snarled through gritted teeth.

"Make sure that no one goes in and out of that room, except the wife," Alex growled. "I don't know what you were thinking, Arun, you idiot! I told you to take care of that nosy friend and Dr. Pettigrew—I meant finish them off, not make them comfortable in a closet."

"I'm sorry, Mr. Becker, sir." Arun cast his eyes to the ground. "What do you want me to do?"

"Well, I need to think. It's a big mess now with more police crawling all over the hospital than there were when Dr. Thornton was brought in after his 'accident.' It's so unfortunate he survived that."

Arun stayed silent while Alex stood staring out his window.

"At least we were able to move the lab quickly, with Abdul's help." He chuckled. "I'm sure he's not enjoying the grilling he must be getting from his wife."

"No, sir," Arun mumbled.

"Well, the first thing I need you to do is get rid of this." Alex pulled a large stone carving of a bear from his desk drawer and cupped it in his huge hands. "I've wiped it clean but there could still be traces of blood, so we have to get rid of it." He sighed and shook his head. "It's one of my favorites from my Arctic collection, but it can't be helped." He handed it to Arun. He sighed again and reached for the kintsugi bowl. He had seen the expression on Nala's face when Malik was holding it. "Better take this too. Such a pity. And, this." He pulled a black balaclava from his desk drawer and handed it to Arun who was already juggling the carving and bowl.

"Yes, sir." Arun looked at the items in his hands and back at the CEO. "Where do you want me to take them?"

"I want you to dispose of them!" Alex grabbed his shoulder and spun him toward the door. "I don't care where, just do it."

Arun stumbled then nodded at his boss. He cradled all three objects in one arm to open the door, and there was Abdul Abadi looming in the doorway.

"That will be all, Arun," Alex said, dismissing him.

"Hello, Abdul." He waved his visitor in. "Good of you to come."

Abdul descended on Alex like a swarm of angry bees. "You smug bastard!" He shook his fist in Alex's face. "You have put me in a very precarious position, both with my wife and with the ministry. I can placate Nala, but the ministry is another matter. There had better not be any more screwups, like the botched attempt at the ski hill. Honestly, what you were thinking? We could have taken care of that more delicately, transferred him to another hospital or just had him fired. If anyone finds out about this . . . this *selling of organs*," he hissed, "you will take the fall, not me." Abdul's breath was coming in short rasps. "And the maid, Anu, she's escaped. I was about to take her to the airport and she disappeared. We need to find her and take care of her, for both of our sakes!" He shook his fist in Alex's face.

Alex took one step back but held his ground. He wasn't going to be intimidated. "I assure you, everything will be fine."

"It had better be."

The tall, broad Emirati man leaned in, and Alex could smell the cigar on his breath. He thought he caught a hint of brandy as well. So much for the commitment to Allah to not drink alcohol.

"I should have stopped you the first time you came to me about selling Nala's stem cells to private buyers."

"It's been lucrative for us both," Alex soothed, "and has secured favor with many very wealthy patrons who are counting on us for continued treatments. And now that the lab has been moved, we don't have to worry about Dr. Thornton, no matter what he thinks he knows. Or Dr. Pettigrew and that Morris woman, for that matter." He smiled. "I must say, our idea to convince Nala to hire Carolyn was brilliant. It was opportune that we happened upon her and Frank in a heated argument that day. She was eager to get out from under his supervision. She can both manage the lab and continue getting us access to the stem cells and organs we need for our clients."

"There will be no more! Now that the ministry is watching more closely, the lab must be entirely legitimate. I should never have given you the code to the lab and the vaults. You got greedy and sloppy. It's over!" Abdul turned on his heel and stormed out, slamming the door behind him.

Alex picked up his phone and punched in a number. "Are you at the lab? Get the bags that have been requested so we can finalize the deal. We don't have much time. This last sale will set us up for life. We'll be gone before they even know what's missing. And, we won't have to cut Abdul in this time."

The beeping of machines, sirens, and the hustling of running feet died down and a moment of peace descended. Susan knew it wouldn't last long. She and Frank were still in the exam room with the police officer sitting vigil, arms crossed, staring straight ahead, waiting for Detective Malik to come and relieve him. With his limited English, Susan wasn't even sure he understood that she wanted to speak with his superior, other than the fact that he nodded after she mentioned Malik's name. Frank had drifted off in a drug-induced sleep after hearing the good news that there was no swelling on his brain and no brain bleed. With some rest he would be fine. They would both be fine.

Susan felt her phone buzz and pulled it out of her pocket. It was a text from Anu.

— *May says maids at airport. I think lab moved to hospital annex. I'm at playground. Please come.*

Susan typed a reply:

— *Stay there, but try to stay out of sight. I will come as soon as I can.*

She looked up as the door opened and Detective Malik came in.

"Thank God you're here." She stood up and showed him her phone with Anu's message. "We need to get to the airport and stop those maids from leaving. We need their testimony. And we need to find Carolyn." Susan stopped short of telling him she had overheard the conversation with Becker and Nala.

"*We* don't need to do anything," he replied and turned to the officer and rattled off orders in Arabic, to which the young officer nodded, spun around, and strode out the door. "You are to stay here with Dr. Pettigrew. Another officer will be here in a moment." He punched a number into his phone and spoke in clipped tones. When he was done, he said to Susan, "The ministry hasn't responded to my calls, but I already have a detail searching the entire hospital and will meet them over at the annex now."

Susan knew about the other building on the property, used for conferences, seminars, and other events. She was surprised that they, whoever *they* were, had moved the lab somewhere so close by.

There was a sharp rap on the door, and the detective opened it to another young officer. Malik spoke to him briefly, nodded toward Susan and Frank, then turned back to Susan. "I need to know where this playground is. We'll have to bring this woman in for questioning, again. She seems to be the common thread here."

"Oh, please," Susan said, "let me go to her. She's scared and doesn't know who she can trust."

"Very well," he replied. "But you will go with a plain-clothes detective. Wait here for now. I'll be back."

"What's going on?" Frank had awoken but was still quite groggy.

"We may have found the maids, including Anu's friend May."

Frank fell back asleep, and Susan sat on the gurney, crossed her legs, and started breathing deeply through her nose to lower her heart rate and head off the brewing panic attack.

~

Alex Becker watched out of his office window as the police swarmed the annex.

"Shit," he said under his breath.

He stood frozen in place and prayed that his accomplice had gotten out with what they needed. He shook himself and started cramming things into his briefcase, including Dr. Thornton's phone. He hadn't been able to get into it, so he didn't know if there was anything incriminating on it, but he didn't give a shit. He would just destroy the SIM card anyway and toss it all into the creek on his way out of town.

~

Malik came back into the exam room shaking his head. Susan unwound her legs from the lotus position and stood up. She waited.

"Come with me," Malike said and motioned for her to follow him.

Susan looked back over her shoulder at Frank, who was sound asleep. She picked up her pace to keep up with the detective. He led her out the front door of the hospital and across the parking lot toward the annex. Two officers were exiting the building, each holding one arm of a woman in handcuffs.

Susan smiled.

"Do you recognize that woman? Have we found Carolyn?"

"Why yes, you have." Her intuition had been right. "That's Carolyn. I guess when she said she had left for a better position, it wasn't at another hospital after all."

They watched as the policemen guided Carolyn into the back seat of the patrol car.

"She was just caught in the lab, filling a cooler with items from a very large refrigerator."

"She seemed like such a rule follower. I guess greed is a strong motivator."

"How did you know she was involved?" Malik asked.

Susan told him how she had run into Carolyn and Anu at the Gold Souk and that Dr. Thornton had mentioned that a nurse had seen him trying to get in the lab.

Carolyn glared at Susan from the back seat of the cruiser.

"Seems Miss Anu is a big piece of the puzzle," Malik said. "Carolyn has implicated her, but we already knew she was involved." He paused. "And, someone else."

"Oh? Who?" Susan asked.

Malik looked over to the front entrance of the hospital where Alex Becker was being brought out in handcuffs as well.

"The CEO? Becker? What does he have to do with this?"

"We're still putting the pieces together, but I think your friend Anu will be able to fill in some of the blanks. Come on," Malik said. "I'm going to take you to the playground myself."

He led Susan to an unmarked car and opened the passenger door for her.

<h1 style="text-align:center">CHAPTER
TWENTY-SIX</h1>

It was dusk by the time Susan and Detective Malik pulled up to the curb next to the playground. Susan hoped Anu would still be there. She wasn't answering Susan's texts.

"Can you wait here until I find her?" Susan asked. "The poor girl is probably petrified, and I don't want her spooked. You can see the playground from here. I'll sit on the bench in full view and wait for her."

"Okay, fine," Malik agreed.

"I'll give you a wave when she's calm and ready to talk with you."

"Don't forget, she's an accomplice and I should be putting her in handcuffs."

"I'm hoping you won't." Susan looked him square in the eye. "She has information we—you—need." He leaned back on the headrest and Susan continued. "You must know that many of these girls come here promised a better life and then are abused and have their passports taken from them. I'm sure Anu did what she felt she had to do to survive."

He grunted, which she took as acknowledgment. She got out of the car before he could change his mind and walked toward the benches on the far side of the playground, which at first glance looked deserted. Then she caught some movement out of the corner of her eye. She turned to see Anu crawling out from under the slide. The young woman looked from side to side before she stood up and made her way over. Susan gathered her in her arms. Anu leaned against her and went limp. Susan wrapped her arms more tightly around her and held on.

"You're safe now," she whispered in her ear.

She hoped she was telling Anu the truth and that they would go easy on her—she hated the thought of the young woman in a jail cell.

It was going to be a long night. Susan knew Detective Malik would eventually take Anu to the station to take her official statement. But relief washed over her. She hoped it wasn't premature.

Nala lay in bed listening to the call to prayer and waiting for the morning light to peek through the gap she left in the blackout curtains. She loved to wake up at dawn and say her own prayers. She didn't go to mosque anymore. She had gotten out of the habit while away at university, but Abdul often went. She hoped he had gone this morning.

She hadn't slept a wink, and her head was throbbing from the fatigue and anger at Abdul for betraying her. They certainly hadn't been a love match, but she had honestly felt there was a mutual respect. How wrong she was. Part of her anger she directed at herself for being so naive and letting her guard down. She could picture in her mind the files she'd left out on the desk in her home office, more than once. She should have locked them in the cabinet. She would visit her father and ask him go to the ministry on her behalf. Surely he would side with her.

She called out for Isa, knowing she would be waiting just on the other side of the door, ready to cater to her every need. And where was Anu? Nala would have to get Isa to look after the children, at least until Anu came back. But that could wait until after she had had her bath and breakfast. If they woke early, the children would play quietly in their rooms until someone went to get them. Isa could bring them down to breakfast after Nala had eaten. She needed to think and didn't want to be distracted.

As she was letting the water out of the tub, there was a tentative knock on the door.

"Yes, what is it?" Nala called.

"Madame," Isa said through the door, "your father is here, and he has another man with him."

"My father?" Nala's blood ran cold. What could he possibly want at this hour of the morning?

"Your husband is back from prayers as well. They are in the dining room having breakfast and have asked for you to join them."

"Thank you, Isa. Tell them I'll be right down. Please lay out my blue kaftan and hijab before you go." With a male visitor in the house, a non-family member, she would need to be fully covered.

"Yes, ma'am."

~

Susan hurried down the corridor to Barry's room. Running on adrenaline and about three hours' sleep, she couldn't wait to fill her friends in. Anu was staying at Susan's, and Susan had left her sleeping soundly. The poor girl was an exhausted wreck after the ordeal she'd been through. Susan knew she would sleep for a while, but she didn't want to leave her alone for very long. After Anu had given her statement, Detective Malik released her into Susan's custody. In exchange for Anu's written testimony, he had promised to organize her safe return home to Sri Lanka. Anu could stay with Susan until the travel arrangements had been worked out.

Her phone buzzed and she paused to look at the screen. Her face turned hot. It was a text from Mitch.

— Just checking in . . . I'm still in Bangkok, home soon.

Susan stood with her jaw agape. Was he kidding? She wasn't going to answer his insensitive, tone-deaf message. He could stew in his guilt. She hit delete.

As Susan turned the corner to Barry's room she saw there was no longer a security guard stationed outside his door. She knocked quietly and pushed the door open. Barry was sitting up in bed with Pat in a visitor's chair on one side and Frank on the other.

"Jesus, Susan." Frank jumped up. "What's happened? We haven't heard a thing, and there's no sign of any police on hospital grounds anymore."

Pat had walked over to her and gave her a big hug. "Are you okay? You got your hair cut."

Susan nodded. "I went to the police station with Detective Malik and Anu, and since I wasn't allowed in the interview room, I went to a hair salon on the same block as the police station and finally got my hair cut off." She didn't give a shit anymore what Mitch would think. It was so much cooler on her neck, and she didn't have to tie it up. "I'm so sorry I didn't text, but it was such chaos and then my phone died . . ." She leaned in for another hug. She needed someone to prop her up after having been the "strong" one for several tumultuous weeks. Her knees almost buckled as Frank took her arm and led her to the cot against the wall.

"They must have given me a sedative in the ER last night," he said. "When I woke up, you were gone and so was the officer."

Barry chuckled. "Ha, now you know how it feels."

"Touché," Frank replied. "Okay, Susan, fill us in. I'm supposed to go to the station later and give a statement."

"So much has happened, I don't even know where to start." Susan rubbed her eyes then ran her fingers through her short curls. The swelling at the back of her head had gone down considerably.

"Frank has caught us up on what happened when you took Detective Malik to the lab . . . the one that's not there anymore." Barry let out a whistle. "What a crazy story!"

"It gets worse," Susan said.

"Worse than a secret lab harvesting stem cells and organs from maids who are being kept against their wills before being deported? Worse than you and Frank being attacked when you saw too much?" Barry said. "And someone trying to kill me because they thought I knew too much? I still don't even really know what I know."

"Well, maybe not worse, but there's more." Susan took a breath and began. "When your CEO found out about Nala's research lab, he started stealing stem cells and organs and selling them to private buyers."

"You're shitting me!" Barry said.

Speechless, Frank just shook his head and dropped back into his chair.

"I shit you not." Susan chuckled then grimaced. "Nothing to laugh about, I'm sorry."

"Go on," Pat urged her.

"Well, apparently Nala's husband was in on it too, and so was Carolyn."

"The same Carolyn that was head nurse here?" Frank said, his eyes wide.

"The one and only," Susan said. "I had run into her and Anu in the Gold Souk when my friend was visiting, and they made up some story about having just bumped into each other. Then I saw Anu cross the street and meet up with another maid, her friend May. And, Pat, remember the time we saw the two women in Barry's hallway and we were sure one of them was Anu?"

"Yes, I remember. And then Carolyn came out of the doors leading to the restricted area."

"We asked if it was your maid she'd been talking with, and she claimed it was one of the hospital cleaners who had gotten lost. She was acting so strange and seemed way too agitated at us for wandering the halls. It just didn't sit well with me. So, I told Detective Malik I suspected Carolyn was involved. Just now, they caught her coming out of the annex, where the lab had been moved, with a cooler full of frozen stem cells."

"Wait, back up. What was Anu doing with Carolyn?" Pat asked.

Susan explained how Nala had coerced Anu and even paid her to help with securing the maids who were forced to have abortions, and for some of them, have organs harvested.

"Nala actually hired Carolyn to work in the lab, not knowing that she was also working with Becker to help steal some of the organs and stem cells and sell them on a black market.

"The stem cells Carolyn was holding when the police caught her were for their most recent buyer. She tried to tell them that she worked at the lab for Nala and was transporting the stem cells for her, but when that didn't fly, she gave Becker up immediately. Becker and Carolyn have been arrested for basically creating a black market for organs and stem cells."

"Holy shit! It was probably Becker who orchestrated my accident. I guess I was drawing too much attention to the lab and putting his big money scam in danger. And, when the fall didn't kill me, he tried to finish the job." Barry shook his head, and there was silence while everyone grappled with the scale of Becker's greed. "We should probably share that with the police, if they haven't figured it out already."

"Absolutely," Frank agreed. "If he's the one who arranged for the explosion on the chairlift, he could be charged with murder as well as attempted murder."

Susan shivered. "It's just too much to process. My head is spinning, and it's not just the concussion!"

"So," Frank continued, "how did you figure out where the maids were?"

"Anu heard from May—the friend she met up with in the Gold Souk. May wound up being one of Nala's 'donors.' I saw her when I snuck into the lab. May texted Anu to say she had been released from the lab when they moved it, and Anu texted me. May told Anu the lab had been moved to the hospital annex." Susan stood and walked to the foot of Barry's bed.

"Anu has given a formal statement admitting her role in

the whole thing. She identified Becker in a lineup as the person who tried to smother Barry and then knocked her down. She realized that he was one of the men she had seen coming down the beach the day of the break-in at Pat and Barry's. She told the police about your file, Barry, and the missing pages. I'm sure the police will want to talk to you more about that."

"I'm sure they will." Barry shook his head. "Was her friend Sara in the ward with the other maids?"

"No, there's still no sign of her." Susan sighed.

"What I don't understand is why Anu would get involved in the first place. And how? I thought she was happy working for us," Pat said.

Susan took a deep breath before replying. "Initially, I think Anu thought she was doing the right thing, helping young women deal with unwanted pregnancies. Then Nala persuaded her to help turn the girls into organ donors by explaining that they would be 'compensated' for their 'donations.' Nala was paying her a lot of money, and Anu was sending it home to her family. Seems Anu had also been pressured into working with Nala's husband, Abdul, without Nala's knowledge. Abdul was helping Becker access the stem cells and organs and was getting a cut of the money. I don't think Nala or Abdul ever thought that Anu would rat them out and jeopardize her own personal and financial security. They played on her strong religious beliefs too." She paused. The others were listening in stunned silence.

"Even though Nala's husband was in on it, I'm not sure she knew about the private buyers," Susan continued. "But she was certainly responsible for kidnapping the maids and using them for her research." Susan let out a long breath.

"Given their extensive connections, chances are Nala and Abdul won't get any jail time."

"We may never find out anyway," Frank said. "It's just too bad that Nala's good work has been tainted by both her and her husband's greed—his for money and hers for fame."

TWENTY-SEVEN

It had been several days since Anu left, and Susan hadn't heard anything other than a text to let her know she had arrived safely in Sri Lanka. It was just as well. They had finally found out what happened to her other friend, Sara, when Anu was asked if she could identify a Jane Doe in the morgue. Turned out Sara had died from complications during the organ harvesting surgery. Anu had wanted to put the whole sordid affair behind her and get on with her life. So did Susan.

She continued going through the clothes in her closet, trying to cull down before the daunting task of packing everything to leave. She and Mitch had had a long heart-to-heart, and he had admitted that he didn't love her anymore. Susan fluctuated between devastating heartbreak and anger. It was going to take some time to process this implosion of her life, but she would be fine. Eventually.

She picked her beloved, well-worn jean jacket up off the closet floor. It still had blood on it from the attack on her and Frank. Tears spilled as she ran her thumb over the peace sign her mother had embroidered on the collar. She should just throw it out—the blood would probably never come out—but she couldn't bring herself to get rid of it; it was one of the few things of her mother's she still had. She should have soaked it in cold water as soon as she had gotten home that day, but she had been exhausted and completely wrung out. She didn't even remember tossing it there.

Her phone buzzed and she looked down to see a FaceTime call coming in from her Aunt Margaret. She punched the answer button.

"Hello, my darling," her aunt said. "I've been thinking about you and thought now might be a good time to have a chat. Are you okay?"

"Oh, I've been better." Susan plunked down on her bed and wiped the tears from her cheeks. "It's good to see you. I just wish it was in person."

"I'm so sorry to hear about you and Mitch. When I got your email I had to see you rather than just hitting reply."

"I'm sorry I told you in an email, but it was easier to get it out that way." Susan started to tear up. "I knew if I called I would lose it."

"You don't need to be strong for me, sweetheart. You can let it out. You've been through a lot in the last few months. You're a strong woman, but it's the strong ones who tend to suffer silently. You know I'm here for you, day and night, 24-7."

"I know, and I appreciate that. You always have been, since I was little."

"Well, you're going to need to go somewhere to regroup," Margaret said. "And I have just the place with just the right person."

"Oh? Where would that be and with whom?"

Margaret smiled. "With me . . . in Paris!"

~

"So, that's the plan—I'm going to France!" Susan raised her glass to her dinner hosts, Pat and Barry, and fellow guests, Frank, Wanda, Joan, and Joan's husband, Brad. Wanda's husband, Harold, was on a layover but had made Susan promise to catch him up when he got back. She took another sip of wine. "I'm going to pack everything up, put it in storage, and then meet my aunt in Paris and sit at sidewalk cafés and eat baguettes and drink Bordeaux for a few months. She just bought a little apartment in the 8th arrondissement *and invited me to stay with her for as long as I like.*"

"I'll drink to that, although I'll miss you." Pat raised her glass and clinked Susan's.

"We will too," added Wanda.

Everyone agreed and clinked glasses.

"Well, you'll all have to visit." Susan took a sip of her wine.

"I'll drink to that too, but we can't go till I get these casts off!" Barry said, raising his glass. He had finally been released from the hospital and was continuing his recuperation at home, without worrying about a threat on his life. "And let's drink to this whole mess finally being cleared up."

"Cheers!" Frank said and took a sip. "I still can't believe it was Alex Becker who tried to smother Barry."

"Thank goodness Anu recognized him in the police lineup. And thank goodness she walked in on him when she did!" said Susan.

"And the police finding Barry's phone in Becker's brief-case when they arrested him clinched it," said Frank. "I guess he figured he'd be on a plane and long gone before they caught up to him."

"This is all so unbelievable," Brad said. "It should be made into a movie."

"I'd rather put it all behind me," Frank said.

"Cheers to that." Pat raised her glass again.

"So, before I tell you all the rest . . . in the spirit of putting everything behind us, I have to apologize to you, Frank," Susan said.

"Apologize? For what?" Frank asked.

"Well, for a while there I was sure you were in cahoots with Nala," Susan began. "When we first met, I really didn't like you. You were so abrupt and, I'm sorry, but you weren't very nice to the nurses."

Frank sighed. "I know, and I feel bad about that. But I was stressed and stretched to my breaking point. Two of my surgical team, Barry and Chris, were out of commission, and then . . ." He paused and inhaled deeply. "Well, you know what happened. We lost Chris."

"I know, and that's why I struggled with my suspi-cions," Susan said. "But then I saw you outside the lab with Nala and also having a conversation with Becker and a guy from the ministry. You can't blame me for being suspicious."

"There was a point where I was suspicious of you too," Barry admitted.

"Well, now you know I was in the dark as much as you were. I just happened to be there when Becker and the ministry guy—Nala's husband—were there. They told me they had business to discuss that didn't concern me. I didn't give it a second thought. My department is only one of many in the hospital so I excused myself and they went off to Becker's office."

"Yes, we know now and I feel bad about it but it's all in the past and we can finally move on," Susan said and raised her glass in the air.

"Amen to that," Pat said.

"Go on, Susan," piped in Joan. Everyone turned to her. "Well, I mean, now that you've cleared the air and all, we're dying to hear the rest."

Susan laughed. "Fair enough." She took a deep breath. "Okay, so when the police searched Becker's office they found the missing pages from Barry's files, including a photo of Becker speaking with one of the couriers," said Susan. "That and finding Barry's phone in Becker's possession was pretty much the clincher in pinning him with the first attempt on Barry's life, at the ski hill."

"Jeez, don't remind me." Barry shuddered.

"Sorry." Susan and Frank apologized in unison and laughed.

"Why didn't you tell us right from the beginning about that photo you had of Becker?" Susan asked.

"I didn't want you to be in danger too. I didn't know what was going on or whether the fact he was talking to the courier indicated that he was involved in anything nefarious. As the hospital CEO, I figured he had every right to know what was going on. I didn't realize the notes on Sara would be in any way related. But now that I think about it, I had asked Becker's secretary for a list of hospital administrators to call and told her I was checking hospitals for a missing friend of my maid's. It's frightening to think Becker was that dangerous."

"I'm thinking it wasn't likely Becker who actually

planted the explosive device on the chairlift; no doubt he hired someone to do that," said Brad.

"Probably true," said Susan, "and I'm sure he'll give them up to the police in the hope of a lighter sentence."

"The only loose thread is what in the hell happened to Nala and Abdul," Pat added.

"I guess that's the least of our worries," Barry said. "And, to be quite honest, I don't care."

"So, what is this about an award?" Susan asked and took a bite of her souvlaki. "Isa, this is absolutely delicious, I'll need to get the recipe."

Isa blushed and dropped an awkward curtsy and scurried back into the kitchen.

"I'm so happy she's come to work for us," Pat said. "She's just getting settled and it seems she's not used to being treated kindly. It's like training an abused dog to trust again." She sighed. "Yes, Frank, tell us about this award."

"Well, it seems that when the sheikh was informed about what was going on at the hospital under Nala's 'supervision,' he was irate. He's been pushing to have the laws strengthened that protect expat laborers, especially those who work inside the homes of both locals and expats. When he found out about Susan's assistance in uncovering the reality of what was going on in the lab, he insisted on rewarding her for her bravery."

Susan laughed. "I'm not sure how brave I was. To be honest, I was shaking in my boots half the time. I just knew we couldn't let it go on. Thankfully, we eventually had Detective Malik on our side."

"Yeah, and the janitor!" Frank raised his glass. "A toast to the janitor who found us in the closet. Who knows what would have happened to us if he didn't. We should find out who he is and make sure he gets a raise!"

"Actually, I did find him," said Susan. "His name is Haile and he's from Ethiopia. I wanted to thank him for the both of us. He deserves a raise, for sure."

~

The Majlis at the Ritz was stunning with six-foot-tall floral arrangements that flanked the entryway. Each one featured cascading roses and white lilies. Inside the sitting room, the rows of armchairs had small tables between them, upon which was a purple orchid and a plate of what Susan imagined were the finest dates. Along the front row were coffee urns and small espresso-sized cups placed on low coffee tables at two-foot intervals.

The chairs were starting to fill with dignitaries wearing formal robes with insignias that Susan didn't recognize. Servers moved efficiently between the rows, filling cups and removing used dishes. It was all quite overwhelming.

Members of the police force were at attention at the front of the room and down both sides. Susan caught sight of Detective Malik waving from the front, motioning them to come forward. Susan started up the side and looked behind her to make sure Frank and Pat, pushing Barry in his wheelchair, were following. Pat nodded at her and she continued to make her way to the front.

Susan's heart was in her throat as she approached Detective Malik. "As-salaam alaikum," she said and bowed her head.

The rest of the day was a blur with the pomp and ceremony befitting a special presentation by the sheikh, attended by the head of every ministry, including the minister of health, who praised the doctors for the incredible work they were doing. During the ceremony he announced that the new CEO of the hospital would be Dr. Frank Pettigrew. Frank sat stunned at the news. With Frank's promotion also came a promotion for Barry to head of surgery.

The four of them were positively buzzing from all the excitement as they piled into the limousine that had been sent to transport them to and from the ceremony.

"What just happened?" Frank said, settling back into the plush seating along the side of the limo. He laughed. "I sure hope they don't expect me to give up doing surgery."

"Well, as the boss, that will probably be up to you," Barry suggested.

"My first official order of business will be to give that janitor, Haile, the raise he deserves."

"Did you hear Detective Malik telling me that Nala's husband has been moved to a less prestigious position, in Ajman?" Susan asked. "Seems he'll be working as a clerk at the Ministry of Transportation."

"Is Nala going with him?" Pat asked.

"Malik said that was a condition of their pardon, that they leave quietly and that Nala hand over everything to do with her research, which will continue, all aboveboard, with closer oversight from the Department of Health."

"So, she won't even be charged with kidnapping?" Pat was incredulous. "It figures."

"I think she probably considers her punishment pretty severe," Frank said. "She was just about to announce her findings publicly. In her mind, what she was doing was for the greater good, because of the lifesaving advancements she's made in transplant research."

"Anu told Malik that Nala had also convinced her that the maids were being deported anyway because they had broken the law," added Susan. "She was helping them stay out of jail, and in return they 'helped' her with her research. And they were paid lots of money then sent home better off, in Nala's mind."

"Talk about twisted logic," Barry said. "And what about Anu's friend who died? Collateral damage? I'm sure there were others too."

"We'll probably never know," Susan said.

The others nodded and fell silent.

TWENTY-EIGHT

Susan dug into the bottom of her satchel and pulled out a long-neglected lipstick tube—"Crimson Shine"—and stroked it on her lips. She rolled them together and tilted her head, looking in the mirror and wondering if it suited her any better now that she would be a divorcée. She shook her head, snatched a Kleenex from the box on the counter, and swiped it across her lips. She licked them and scrubbed again with the same Kleenex, smearing what was on it down her chin. She grabbed a paper towel, ran it under the tap, and furiously wiped her lips and chin.

She gripped the counter and closed her eyes as tears rolled down her face. A toilet flushed in a stall behind her. She took a deep breath and brushed the tears away. So much to think about. She would have to spend some time rediscovering herself, who she was on her own, without Mitch, without a career. She would need to do a little rein- venting, but a splash of lip color wouldn't cut it. She would have to dig a bit deeper. That would have to wait, she had a flight to catch. Her stomach fluttered. She tossed the tube of lipstick in the garbage can and pulled a lip gloss from the side zipper pocket, gave her lips a swipe, and popped it in her satchel along with her notebook. *Time with Aunt Margaret is just what I need*, she thought as she headed for the departure lounge.

She wondered how long it would take to quell the butterflies in her belly every time she flew and had to go through immigration. She suspected that Nala had been the one to contact immigration to flag her passport when she went to Bangkok to see Kan. She would never know for sure, but it made sense. It was likely only thanks to Mitch's employer that she hadn't been deported, right or wrong. She didn't think she would ever return to the UAE, so she wouldn't have to worry about that anymore. At least not for a long while. She did still have friends there. Hopefully Pat and Barry, and Wanda, Joan, and their husbands would visit once she got settled wherever she decided to start the next phase of her life as a single woman. There were a lot of changes happening, other than just being single again, and she was looking forward to being in the loving fold of her aunt's arms and just taking a pause.

She chose a seat near the gate, flipped open her laptop, typed in the search bar "private investigator training online," and smiled.

ACKNOWLEDGMENTS

As I approach the release of my latest novel, *Deep Freeze*, the long-awaited second book in the Deep Mysteries series, and the ten-year mark since the publication of the first, *Deep Deceit* (March 8, 2015), I marvel at how fast time passes. In the years since then, I became a full-time caregiver to my mom, while at the same time establishing a hybrid publishing company. I worked from home so it was a win-win. To say I had little time to write is an understatement. In the summer of 2023, we moved my mom into a care home and shortly after, I asked a trusted editor who had been working with me since starting OC Publishing in 2016 to join me as associate publisher, which finally gave me time to do my own writing. It was a spark of an idea that came to us over a beer at The Old Triangle, our favourite pub. Isn't that where the best ideas percolate?

So first, I want to thank my mom, *our* Mother Theresa (MT for short), for always being my sounding board, my champion, my first beta reader, and my biggest fan. She passed away in February 2024 at the age of ninety-nine. She lived a great life, raised five kids (I'm the youngest), had seven grandchildren, and three great-grandchildren. I miss her dearly but feel so fortunate to have been raised by her, that I have many of her characteristics, and that she instilled in me a love of reading and a passion for story-telling. She will always be one of the many badass angels on my shoulder.

The trusted editor that I mentioned is the amazing Marianne Ward, who has become not only my associate publisher, but a dear friend and the editor of this book. I am fortunate to have her leading many OC Publishing projects and especially partnering with me to make the Deep Mysteries as rich and riveting (I hope) as they can be. And, of course, our pub nights that I always look forward to as it obviously triggers the early germination of great ideas.

Thanks to my early readers Bruce Bishop, Janice Friend, Peter Moreira, donalee Moulton, and Vernon Oickle. Your feedback was invaluable and your blurbs greatly appreciated.

Finally, thank you to all my family and friends who cheer me on and are always on deck to help at book fairs and launches (my brother Paul, sister-in-law Violet, niece Marianne, and BFFs, Pam and Barb), or to be sounding boards as industry experts (my sister Janet the nurse and brother Peter the medic), or just to listen and pour the wine when things get too overwhelming (my sister Sue). I formally dedicated this book to MT, but it's for all of you as well, including beloved readers, indie author supporters, and fellow authors.

Now work begins on the third book in the Deep Mysteries Series, *Deep River*, which will be set in Paris. I'll be heading there to do research and participate in the renowned Rohm Literary Paris Writers Retreat in May 2025. I'm usually the one leading the workshops, so this will be a treat.

ABOUT THE AUTHOR

Anne Louise O'Connell
Author, Editor, Publisher
Anne Louise O'Connell grew up in Halifax, Nova Scotia, and has lived around the world, escaping the cold of Canada on a hunt for warmer climes, with stops in Florida, Dubai, and Thailand. In 2007, after seventeen years in the PR business, she decided to focus on her real passion and just write. In 2016, after working as a freelance copywriter and writing coach, and writing three books, she returned to her hometown and established OC Publishing.

In addition to being a partner/hybrid publisher working with authors internationally, O'Connell is a multi-genre author who has written both fiction and nonfiction. Her first novel, *Mental Pause*, won an IPPY (Independent Publisher Magazine) Book Award. Her second novel, *Deep Deceit*, is the first in the Deep Mysteries Series. Her nonfiction books include *@Home in Dubai . . . Getting Connected Online and on the Ground* (Summertime Publishing, UK); a collection of her expat living and travel stories titled *Swimming with the Elephants and Other Adventures;* and a co-published collection titled *Phuket Island Writers–An Anthology of Short Stories* (both fiction and nonfiction).

In her role as publisher, O'Connell loves to mentor first-time authors, does developmental editing, and assists others in developing their author platforms, while liaising with professional editors and designers throughout the publishing process. The genres she publishes include: women's fiction, historical fiction, mystery/suspense, memoir, YA, middle grade, first chapter books, and children's picture books.

While living in Thailand, Anne was a contributing writer for *The Wall Street Journal Expat Blog* and *Global Living Magazine* and a regular columnist for *Expat Focus*. O'Connell is a two-time graduate of Mount Saint Vincent University: Early Childhood Education (1984), hence her love of children's literature, and a Bachelor of Public Relations (1990).

Connect with Anne:
 Website: www.ocpublishing.ca
 YouTube channel: www.youtube.com/OCPublishing
 Facebook: www.facebook.com/ocpublishing
 LinkedIn: www.linkedin.com/in/annelouiseoconnell
 Instagram: www.instagram.com/ocpubhfx
 TikTok: www.tiktok.com/@ocpubhfx